Naughty Girls' Erotic Taboo Sex Stories

Explicit Fantasies for Adults. Orgasmic Threesome, First Time Lesbian, BDSM, Cuckolds, Roleplay, Anal Sex, Bedtime Dirty Talking & Sex Positions.

Janice Foxx

Table of Contents

Secret Lessons

Jeanette was very nervous and restless. Her last unit test results were unexpected and unfortunate containing a multitude of red marks and a big fat F in the corner. If she failed her mathematics and science classes, she would be in academic debacle, and her GPA would decline enough that she'd lose her scholarship and eventually make her a college dropout. Jeanette couldn't afford the extortionate fees without assistance, and her parents were too financially distressed to help with her tuition. She shifted her weight from foot to foot restlessly, moving apprehensively outside her Dean's office, waiting impatiently for him to welcome her inside.

Jeanette was a charming youthful college girl. She was a freshman, just turned nineteen, with an attractive figure and long dark-brown hair. Behind her glasses, she had bright blue eyes with long lashes. She had a slightly mousy, bibliophile look, youthful and innocent. She was a studious young girl, hard-working and diligent. However, her intelligence inclined more toward literature than Math, and she was having a hard time putting forth a concentrated effort to that subject. Between her class load and the employment that she'd taken to manage and meet her ends financially, she was discovering school to be difficult; no medications, alcohol and wild sex for Jeanette. She was fortunate if she even got a free night to mingle with friends and peers.

Dean Marcus Ortiz opened the door, running his eyes over the mousy young lady standing apprehensively before him. He took in her ample, succulent bosoms and her wide hips; noticed the way in which she meekly looked down like she couldn't force herself to meet his eyes. He grinned fleetingly - he definitely knew why Jeanette was here to see him, yet he felt that he might have the option to help the young girl if she was prepared and enthusiastically consensual to take a little detour to earn her grades.

"Jeanette," he stated, his voice soft but commanding. "Come in and have a seat. I assume that you're here about the failing grades in the recent unit tests."

Grimacing at the word 'failing grades', Jeanette slipped tentatively into the Principal's office; she sat down opposite him across a large oak desk. For a moment, her troubled mind was mesmerized by Mr. Ortiz's hunky physique. He looked so young compared to other teachers and professors in the college. He had a strong, brawny build, with a broad chest and wide shoulders. He had thoughtful grey eyes that wrinkled around the sides as he grinned. There was some salt in his brown hair, yet with his authoritative voice and his English accent, he was the secret fantasy of many girls in the college, Jeanette's very own included. She blushed and looked away, concealing her yearning eyes by looking down at her clasped hands.

"I-yes," Jeanette stated in her usual calm voice.

"I just... I can't fail in my grades, Sir. Is there any way I could make it up with some additional credits? I've been diligent, I can't believe I failed. I simply needed more time to work on the projects and assignments. I can't fail, sir. I can't."

The unfortunate and poor, young lady's eyes stung as she tried to stop the tears from falling.

Dean Ortiz just watched her silently for a few minutes. He folded his enormous hands together on his desk.

"Well, if you had put forth a better concentrated effort, as you say you did, we wouldn't be in this position," he stated, shaking his head. "However, I do feel for you. I know your academic and financial situations, and I know beyond all doubt that failing in your primary subjects would ruin your chances of a scholarship. In any case, you should understand that I can't generally favor one student over another, regardless of his or her conditions." He shrugged his wide shoulders regretfully.

Jeanette looked crest-fallen and squirmed in her chair, tears streaming down her cheeks as she sobbed, slouching in on herself. "I'm sorry," she said. "I'll improve, I promise. What will I do? I won't be able to bear the cost of my studies; I'll become a dropout. My parents will be so disappointed. Isn't there any way? I'll do anything." Jeanette begged in her desperation.

Those sweet words, yet earnest pleas were music to Mr. Ortiz's ears when he gazed at the helpless, yet honest student. The Dean could feel his cock throbbing just from watching her cry. Reaching under his desk, he gave himself a speedy squeeze as he watched her, pretending that he was wondering and reviewing his options. After a little delay, he grinned mischievously.

"Well," he stated, "You have an option. I believe that you're simply in need of a desperate... direction. A little counsel. Somebody to deal with your time all the more efficiently and ensure you study equally for your classes. Somebody to punish you, if the need be."

Jeanette gulped hard and looked up; her face was reddened from crying. She twisted her hands restlessly in her lap, meeting her Dean's eyes quickly before looking down at his huge oak desk. "P-punish me?" she was bewildered, her voice shaking.

"Indeed, punish you," Dean Ortiz stated. "Make you accountable for your activities. Or on the other hand, I think, I can simply fail you. I surmised your education meant more to you than that, but," He shrugged nonchalantly and reclined in his seat.

"No! No, I need you to... direct me... counsel me," Jeanette stated, nodding her head. "I'm truly inefficient in my time management. Perhaps if you make me up a timetable or something...you know to manage my time and make up for my loss."

"Oh, my dear, I'm willing to give you much more significant motivation than a timetable," the Dean stated, grinning like a shark. "Lock the door."

Jeanette moved apprehensively, appearing as though she wanted to protest. After a long minute, she surrendered and nodded her head. Standing on shaky legs, she shuffled over to the main door, bolted it before returning and standing anxiously by the large oak desk, waiting patiently for further guidance.

Dean Ortiz watched her. Jeanette was wearing a charming, knee-length skirt. He loved skirts. Simple access, always. "Why don't you sit down?" he chuckled, pulling open a desk drawer. He brought forth a root of ginger and a knife, and set about peeling and cutting it before her. "Do you recognize what this is?" he inquired mildly.

"Uh," Jeanette observed nervously, chills moving down her spine, her fingers felt abnormally cold, and she felt unquenchably thirsty as the spicy smell kept on hammering her sensitive nostrils, while her Dean carved the root. "Ginger?" she swallowed hard, her eyes glancing up at his face, desperately seeking approval.

"Bingo," the Dean exclaimed, grinning momentarily as he worked. "Ginger. There's an old practice, back in Japan. While receiving a caning, the subject can clench their butt cheeks to alleviate the agony. Teachers introduced ginger as a way to ensure that those needing discipline encountered the torment of it absolutely. Inserted into the anus, it delivers a blistering burning sensation which just strengthens as the subject clenches." As he talked, he worked, crafting the ginger into an impeccable butt plug.

Jeanette went cold; she felt her fingers chilling like ice, and her heart and stomach doing summersaults, her throat closing. Her eyes snapped from her Dean's face to the ginger he was carving and back again, desperately trying to sense if he was kidding. She blushed. Her lips parted slightly, her breathing and her pulse increased. She was suddenly mindful of her sensitive bosoms, her nipples hardening and grazing her bra. "You... please don't do that," she pleaded as her eyes widened. "I-I could report you about this unacceptable and unethical behavior!"

"Yes, indeed," the Dean responded mischievously, putting the recent and just perfectly crafted ginger butt plug on his desk. "Certainly, you can report about this so-called 'unacceptable and unethical behavior' to the administration. But if you do that, you would and could fail the unit tests for sure." He chuckled deviously, that hard smile on his face shot jolts of electricity down her spine. Jeanette trembled like a dry leaf in a whirlwind. "Moreover, can you make anyone believe your version of the story? Your word against mine. It's a lot easier to accept that a bitchy student has an issue with getting an F than for a respected Dean to be administering corporal punishment." He wiped his hands on a hand towel and gazed at the young lady sitting opposite him. "You can leave if you want to fail in the unit tests and have your scholarship application dismissed. Or on the other hand, you can come here and bend over my knee. It's your choice, sweet little girl." He reclined on his office chair and pushed it away from his desk exhibiting his brawny thighs. There was a slight lump down one leg, his cock throbbing in his pants.

Refusing to stare at her Dean, Jeanette vacillated for a minute. She ran a trembling hand through her hair and inhaled deeply. He had her, and she knew it. She realized that if she left his office, she could bid farewell to her college degree. Maybe she desperately sought what he was offering. Maybe if he disciplined her, instructed her, she could improve. Flicking her eyes up, she gazed anxiously at the ginger butt plug, her ass cheeks clenching at the intriguing, yet the depraved idea. Then, reluctantly, she got to her feet. She ambled over to him, her legs powerless and trembling, battling to maintain her balance. Her heart pounded like bass drums. She could sense the blood pounding in her ears. Her face felt like it was set ablaze, and she was troubled, yet aroused to realize that she was wet. After one long and final pause, she warily bent over her Dean's lap that was firm as a board.

"That's my good girl," Dean Marcus Ortiz expressed, letting his hand settle on her warm ass, caressing her through her skirt. He moved in his seat before adjusting her on his lap, pulling and pushing until she was resting over his thighs, her bubble butt up in the air, her crotch squeezed firmly against one of his hunky thighs. "I must have your hands," he commanded in a calm voice while loosening his tie. Then he pulled it free. "A young lady like you, a bitch girl like you, I bet you've never been spanked appropriately. I won't let you interfere and spoil this disciplinary session."

Jeanette flushed. Dean Ortiz was spot on. She had never been spanked. She gasped desperately, feeling intimately mindful of her body as she reached her hands behind her, allowing him to take them and bind them firmly behind her back with his tie. She could feel his warm thigh against her crotch, the blood racing to her head as he pushed down on her back, angling her rear end up in the air. Her breath came in pants as she wriggled.

When he'd secured her hands, Dean Ortiz wasted no time in lifting her skirt. He grinned wickedly at the wet spot on her white panties, running his fingers over it softly, feeling Jeanette bounce and twitch against him. "Perhaps this won't be such a punishment after at all," he chuckled. "You're so wet that you've soaked through your underwear. Perhaps this is what you craved for from the beginning, hmm? Someone to take control and make you responsible for your actions? You aren't the first student that I've had to discipline. Nor will you be the last." Stripping her panties down gradually over her magnificent thighs, Dean Ortiz uncovered her smooth, round butt cheeks. That ass would be cherry red when he was done with it. He stroked her smooth round butt firmly before sliding his fingers down, slipping between her folds. She was so smooth and hot against his fingers, so welcoming to him when he hadn't even started playing with her yet.

"Please don't, Sir," she cried, jerking on his lap as his fingers caressed her wet cunt. "Please don't touch me there, please. Sir...I beg you...I've never...I'm a virgin." Even as she pleaded to him not to, her clit throbbed against his fingers, her legs twitching when he touched her. There was a thirst somewhere inside her that yearned to be quenched, that pleaded for those fingers to slide somewhere inside her warm, wet pussy.

"But you're so wet," Dean Ortiz teased, sinking one finger inside her easily, ignoring her pleas. "Your mouth says no, but your pussy yearns for cock. It doesn't make any difference if you're a virgin. Virgins can be horny little sluts." The Dean twisted his finger gradually inside her, feeling the way in which this slutty student twitched and gripped around his inspecting fingers. When he faced an obstruction, he paused - no point breaking her cherry with his fingers when he could ultimately break it with his cock.

12

"I'm not," Jeanette whined, trembling in a peculiar blend of embarrassment and twisted desire as he fingered her virgin pussy. She'd hardly investigated herself down there - she had always felt insecure and unassertive about her sexuality. She had never known what to do. She bit down on a groan at the thrilling sensation of his harsh, thick finger within her - if she felt that stuffed with half of his finger inside, she couldn't imagine how someone ever took in a full hardened cock.

Dean Ortiz slipped his finger out of her tight, drenched cunt and smeared it on her butt cheeks. "Right," he said. "Well, if you weren't a slut, you wouldn't be soaked and getting horny when being put over your teacher's lap. You can't trick me - not when I can see precisely how wet you are." He brought his hand down on her round, hemispherical scoop like ass cheek with a resounding slap.

Jeanette winced and clenched, letting out a little squeak. At first, the slap didn't register, but soon, it stung, making her grimace, battling against the tie holding her arms behind her back. Feeling that sting, altered her perspective. "I don't want to do this," Jeanette panted. "You can't make me. Just let me go, I prefer failing...this is too humiliating... I didn't realize, I've changed my mind. I'll tell!"

Dean Ortiz just chuckled. "You think that I'll let you go, now that I have you tied up over my lap? Do you really think I'll release you? Don't make me think that you're such an idiot!" he teased.

"No, I'm not going to release you until I've exacted each ounce of atonement from your perfect skin. I won't stop until your butt becomes flushed a fiery red for me. You can tell whoever you want, or you can acknowledge what's happening to you and pass your semester. But, for each of the subjects you fail, you'd better accept that you'll be back in here having your ass beaten raw. A little agony is far superior to being a college dropout and ending your career dreams, right? Besides, based on how wet your cunt is, I assume you may be getting aroused and enjoying this a bit. Now shut up, bitch."

Gripping her hair firmly, Dean Ortiz opened his desk drawer. He pulled out a gag ball. "For exceptional cases like you," he informed the crying young lady. "This is for those that need some additional consideration and discipline. Don't want something over the top, isn't that right?" He pulled her head back until she opened her mouth to wheeze with the agony. The Dean slipped the gag in place, snapping the ties behind her head and adjusting the restrains until it was nice and tight - there was no chance she could spit it out. The young lady tried desperately to plead something, but was stifled behind the gag. All he could hear was her gasping through her nose and her muffled cries and pleas.

Poor Jeanette was a quite a sight, forced over her Dean's knee, her pale, hemispherical ass mounds up in the air. There was a red impression on her butt - the first of many. Her glorious pink pussy was in a splendid display, her hands bound behind her back, her succulent bosoms full and her chest heaving. She was choked, tears running down her reddened cheeks, her hair, sticking to her brow as she perspired with fear, waiting and dreading what was to come.

"Uh oh," the Dean teased, reaching for the ginger butt plug, "I almost forgot this." He parted her butt cheeks, appreciating her pink, impeccable anal cavity. Clearly this gap had been just as unused as her pussy. He lubed the ginger plug up and squeezed it cautiously against her butt hole. "Keep in mind, the more you clench, the more will be the agony," he stated, shoving the plug brutally inside her. He'd left two knots - one to keep the ginger anchored in her, and one outwardly to prevent it from slipping too far into her. He shoved it up to the second bunch, positioning the ginger a few inches inside her ass.

Jeanette snorted as she felt something being thrust into her butt hole. It was the first time that she'd ever had anything shoved into that cavity, and it stimulated and repelled her all at once. She'd read tales about anal play before, and she'd generally been curious, yet she'd never been bold and adventurous enough to touch herself that way. The ginger went in so effectively, extending her a bit, about the size of a finger. She groaned into the gag, her body straining, her pussy throbbing and clenching like it needed something to fill it up, as well. Then, the burning started. It began as a slight shiver that developed into a sting.

She couldn't resist clenching around the ginger plug, and that simply aggravated it, making it burn. She felt as if her butt hole was set ablaze. Jeanette squirmed on his lap, screaming behind the gag, begging him to take it out.

"Settle down," Dean Ortiz stated, pushing on the small of her back, holding her down. He didn't need her squirming out of position. "The more you fight and grip, the more terrible it'll feel. Now, I'm going to spank you until I'm certain you're truly upset for failing your grades." With that, he began to spank her ass. He'd always favored a hand spanking to anything else. It was quite a lot more intimate and sexual than paddling or a whipping; however, each had its own benefits. At times, he got aroused by the use of a paddle and rested his hand from the sting, but Jeanette was a virgin in every sense of the word. He would need to ease her into it before she could take a decent, hard, over the knee paddling.

He warmed her up gradually, taking as much time as possible. The room resonated with each crack as his palm landed on her exposed, vulnerable ass cheeks. Jeanette whimpered, squirmed, groaned and screamed out behind the gag. While Dean Ortiz thoroughly delighted in the sounds. The gag ensured they were stifled enough not to leave his office.

Jeanette gasped behind the gag. It hurt. It hurt more than anything she'd ever felt. She really wanted to clench each time he spanked her bare bottom, and that simply caused the ginger root in her ass to burn a thousand times more terribly. She cried helplessly, feeling her ass warm and sting as he spanked her. But the torment wasn't the worse part. What was truly terrible was that each hard smack drove her crotch down, scouring her clit against his hard thigh. She groaned and battled against the restraints around her wrists helplessly, yet intensely animated as he spanked her. Her clit throbbed in accordance with her heartbeat, her nipples scouring against her bra with each excruciating hard blow, sending waves of electric sensation through her. In any event, being so vulnerable, gagged and bound stimulated her. Each time she pulled against her ties she gasped with sensual excitement and passionate anticipation.

"That moment...you know that one...the first grasp...being claimed...taken...adored...and your heart beats just a little faster...and your mind swirls with pleasure..." Jeanette's mind was shocked with the realizations of her perverted fantasies.

After two or three minutes of warm-up, the devious Dean stopped, scouring his hand over her stinging, hot ass mounds. "You take on great color," he praised, giving the ginger plug a little contort, feeling her shiver against him, hearing her muffled cries. He slid his fingers down, laughing at how wet she was. She was so well lubricated by her own excitement juices that he didn't need to shove his finger in – she was dribbling. He spread her lips to devour the magnificent view, adorning the dewy wetness. " I see you like it significantly more than I expected.

That's great. I've been searching for a whore bitch to keep for quite a while. You're beginning to seem as though you fit the bill. I love it when my whores get wet from the abuse, I give them. You ready, darling? Since that was only the warm-up."

Jeanette's first reaction was a stifled whine. She shivered as he spread her open and saw her, flushing with shame at how wet she was. She couldn't resist. Possibly it was her virginity, or perhaps it was the way this fulfilled each profound, dark, twisted and perverted fantasy she had; however, even the way in which he treated her, stirred her. She heaved in a breath through her nose, trembling on his lap, her rear end ablaze. Tears stung her eyes as she waited for him to begin once more, yielding and surrendering to her destiny.

His will was her mandate. His hands were her thirst. His essence was her drink. His focus was her pleas. His will was her need. His mind was her growth. Her trust was his reward.

"That's it," Dean Marcus Ortiz teased, rubbing her bare bottom with one big hand, feeling how hot her butt was after the vigorous spanking. "There's a decent slut." He swung his hand down with a hard crack, sensing the sting against his palm, laughing deviously as Jeanette's back arched as she squirmed excruciatingly. He fired up a hard, brutal spanking, driving her down with each blow. When he was done with her, her rear end would be so swollen and so dark a red that it would look purple. "His spell is powerful, intoxicating, and addictive. You're a butterfly caught in his net, unable and unwilling to escape. You're his...totally his." Jeanette's lust-filled conscience poked her twisted fantasies into her mind.

Jeanette screeched and struggled on his lap, sobbing quietly to herself as he held her down and spanked her fiercely. Whimpering, she shook back and forth, striving to wriggle off his lap. But all she could achieve was crushing herself down against his thigh, boosting her reluctant sensual excitement until she was gasping with pain and pleasure. Each time he hit her, she shuddered and clenched firmly around the ginger butt plug conquering her rear end, burning the sensitive tissues inside her. Snorting, she rocked down against the Dean's thigh, a flood of eternal ecstasy dragged her to the heavenly excitements that conquered her earthly senses. She could feel it invigorating, gradually building and strengthening, her toes curled as she wailed – she realized that once she came, it would be a hundred times more terrible, yet she couldn't stop it. Her muscles bunched up, her body twitched and jerked, her clit throbbed. With piercing moans, Jeanette came, shivering and curving on her Dean's lap, the ginger butt plug invading her anal cavity and her perfect ass mounds practically purple from the vigorous spanking. Her pussy spouted sensual fluids, dribbling it onto his thigh as her stomach clenched and her overwhelming climax exploded through her.

Dean Ortiz just grinned victoriously as he realized the young girl just came against him, twisting, shuddering, and whimpering on his lap. He spanked her more viciously all the time during her sexual release, his hand felt the agony of the continued spanking, his palm felt the terrific heat of the relentless spanking, yet he didn't stop even as Jeanette's whines and groans of ecstatic pleasure transformed into cries of distress. At long last, his hand stilled on her wounded, swollen ass, stroking his own hand imprints, beaten skin with his palm. Reaching for the ginger butt plug, he gave it a little twist, feeling her shiver and jerk against him.

"Now," Dean Ortiz teased. "You can show me how sorry you are as you ride me, or I can spank you until you're ready to regret like the slut you are." He gave her burning, cherry red, sore ass cheeks another vicious sharp slap, the sound of skin against skin reverberating through the room. "What do you say, slut?"

Jeanette just groaned behind the gag. Tears trickled down her reddened cheeks. This wasn't at all how she had imagined losing her virginity, yet she realized that he would simply spank her until she agreed to his terms. She cried as he spanked her once more, harder and more ferocious that the last one, then immediately nodded her approval, breathing hard through her nose.

"Good little slut," Dean Ortiz appreciated. Grabbing her by the hair, he pushed and pulled, peeling her skirt off her and settling her until she was straddling his lap, absolutely naked from the waist down. Jeanette was facing Mr. Marcus, and he gazed at his own reflection in her frightened, beautiful eyes, adoring how vulnerable and helpless, she looked with her mouth gagged and those enormous eyes gushing tears. She gazed at her own reflection in his expressive, sparkling eyes, she shivered at the thought of the inevitable, she sensed her lust corrupting her soul.

"If you attempt to get away, or you don't do as you're told, I'm going to put you over my oak desk and whip you with my belt," he said. "Fuck, I'll whip your streaming, glorious, virgin little cunt if you ever put a foot off the mark." Reaching between them, he pushed her shirt up over her chest, adoring her succulent teenage bosoms. They were ample and perky, smooth and great. Reaching behind her, he unclasped her bra, releasing those juicy milk buckets from their prison so that they bounced and giggled before his hungry lips. The nipples were hard and swollen from her sensual excitement; Jeanette had hardly come down from the highest peaks of lustful excitements.

Taking a pair of scissors from his desk, the Dean sliced through the bra, ignoring Jeanette's whines of dissent. "From now and into the foreseeable future," Mr. Marcus asserted, "If I find you wearing a bra in class, I'll grant you the most pathetic grades, even if you pass." He stripped her bra away. "You have exquisite tits – there's no reason why you shouldn't exhibit them. I'm certain you'll get more attention from younger men. I likewise need you to wear shorts, under the knee skirts without any panties. Consistently. Everybody has to realize what a little perverted slut you are, a deviant little bitch who just orgasmed from a hardcore over the knee spanking. Am I clear?" All Jeanette could do was nod her approval. He left her top, simply hiking it up so he could see her juicy bosoms, superbly round and a decent D cup, topped with pink nipples.

"His lips against yours, filling your body with unquenched desire. Feeling his hot breath against your mouth as he exhales into you. A touch so strong you have to steady your body against his for the fear of falling." Jeanette felt her perverted thoughts poking her sole existence and corrupting her soul.

Sliding his hands up her stomach, the Dean took a bosom in each hand, squeezing them, mauling them with all his strength and kneading over the tight, perky, nipples. He grinned as she panted, leaned forward and sucked in one of her tits into his hungry mouth, rolling the hardened nipple between his teeth, teething just enough to make her pant and arch her back with torment. Electric impulses of lust rushed down Jeanette's spine that produced a tingling effect between her legs. He worked her nipples for a few long minutes, squeezing, tugging, pulling, biting and rolling them expertly in between his lips, tongue, and mouth until they hurt with sensitivity. He would have a fabulous time tying off these ample bosoms and spanking them or clamping the nipples and stretching them until she shouted in an ecstatic blend of pain and pleasure. One more day, maybe.

Poor Jeanette had never truly had someone play with her sensitive and juicy bosoms like this before. Her cheeks burned with embarrassment as he exposed her, fixing her gaze at the wall, trembling like a leaf. The most intimate she had ever been under these current circumstances was when one of the football players had given her bosoms a snappy squeeze while they had been making out. She had pushed him away, rebuffed him saying it was too soon. He'd dumped her a few days later for not putting out. She heaved and groaned throatily, arching her chest into his passionate ministrations, shivering and twitching as he worked her nipples until they became so sensitive that even the faintest brush of his fingers or his tongue made her squirm in pain and pleasure. It was excruciating; however, she ached in such a stirring way, that she really wanted to arch her back and offer him her tits, jerking when he got excessively harsh, recoiling a little when he bit her. However, she couldn't deny that her pussy was soaking wet, that her nipples were hard and yearning for his impassioned and reckless maneuvers.

Breathing in hard, deep and fast, the Dean inhaled her fragrance. He slid a hand between her legs and thrust two fingers inside her, moaning at how wet she was. He could sense her pussy clenching and squeezing around his fingers, desperately attempting to devour him in her lust. The hymen was still intact, and he was anticipating breaking it. Through the slender wall isolating her butt from her pussy, he could sense the ginger butt plug still covered inside her, and he grinned wickedly. Unbuttoning and unzipping his pants with one hand, he pulled his leaking and hardened cock out. Pre-cum spilled from the tip and he moaned, pulling his fingers out of her pussy and replacing it with his cock head.

"I need you to slide your hot cunt down on my dick," he breathed, his cock throbbing excitedly at the idea of sinking into that tight warmth. "You must not stop until it's all the way inside you. I don't care if it hurts you. If you stop, I'll whip your cunt before I fuck it."

"He's responsible for your peaks and valleys, Jeanette. The pulsating waves and earth-shattering releases that you experience the flying the pleasures of the highest heavens. It doesn't matter if you're restrained or not, whether you fuck or make love, he's always in control. In fact, he's in absolute control." Her perverted mind screamed in her ears as goose bumps coursed all over her skin. Jeanette whimpered, sobbing at her sheer helplessness and vulnerability. She could feel his bulbous cock head at her lubricated opening – it appeared to be so much bigger than his fingers. She didn't have the foggiest idea of how she might get it inside her. Breathing deeply through her nose, she begged him with her eyes. However, she realized it was pointless. She moved, dropping herself gradually down on his gigantic, thick cock, feeling it open her up gradually. She winced, breathing hysterically as she cautiously pushed down. It ached, burned, tore her into halves as she attempted to get it in her, and for a moment, she figured she couldn't manage it, yet the idea of him whipping her cunt restored her will. With a muffled scream, Jeanette forced herself down on his big fat dick, feeling something tear inside her, piercing agony travelled through her as she forced herself down until his big fat cock was all the way in her tight, little, streaming, virgin cunt. When he was in her, Jeanette just screamed – there. She had finally lost her virginity. Dean Ortiz had taken it from her.

He just moaned as she squeezed him into her hot, tight, virgin cunt. "Fuck, I always love virgins," his perverted mind screamed inside his head. They were generally so tight, and they got so thoroughly wet. Indeed, even as Jeanette hurt herself for him, her pussy was so tight and wet. Dean Ortiz felt Jeanette's thrust down, his bulbous cock head rocking through her hymen. The devious Dean laid his hands on her glorious hips, helping to ease her down the rest of the length of his bold erection until his balls were squeezed up against her mons, his ten-inch fat manhood buried deep inside her tight womanhood. The Dean groaned and fucked upward, attempting to thrust further.

"That's my good slut," the Dean breathed, slapping her clenched perfect ass. "Now, ride me, as hard as possible. Make your Dean come. Show me how desperate you are to earn your grades and scholarship."

Jeanette whimpered. With her hands bound behind her back, it was difficult to adjust herself for up and down thrust. She could feel his big fat cock throbbing in her aching and delicate pussy. The ginger still burned inside her; however, its fierceness had faded away a little, allowing her to concentrate on how stuffed and full she felt. Her nipples were still hard, and extremely sensitive. Inhaling deeply and fast, her legs quivered, she pushed herself up, feeling his big fat cock move inside her. She inhaled hysterically – it felt like his thick cock was tearing her insides with it. Yet, she ached and yearned for the ecstatic blend of pain and passionate pleasure. This was an out of this world experience which she craved to fulfill, deep within her perverted mind.

"That's too slow for a prime slut," Dean Ortiz snorted. Grasping her hips, he forced her down on his big fat cock, lifting his hips so he could hammer up into her soaking pussy. He moaned as his cock slid inside her warm, wet cunt in one thrust. The feeling was true heaven. "You feel so great, slut." He groaned, beginning to use his grasp on her hips to fuck her in long, powerful strokes. He hammered somewhere inside with each push as if he was attempting to get as deep inside her as he could. Sliding a hand between her legs, he ran his fingers over her swollen clit – Jeanette was still aroused, flying the peaks of excitements from her Dean's hardcore spanking, and she shivered as he touched her, roughly, yet passionately.

Slowly yet steadily, it got easier. Jeanette's aching cunt loosened up somewhat, so wet and smooth from her amorous excitement. Her chest heaved, her body shivering as the Dean fingered her sweet, throbbing little clit. His big fat cock moved against a spot inside her that made her groan behind her gag. Jeanette cried and whimpered as Dean Ortiz took her, shoving into her again and again. Goosebumps raced along her skin, her succulent bosoms bouncing as she slid all over on his thick throbbing erection. Her aching cunt milked his hardened erection. Eventually, she surrendered to the demands of her throbbing clit, pounding down against his fingers each time he shoved that rock-hard cock right inside her.

The Dean felt her climax before she tensed – rigorous and vigorous muscle contractions streamed through her pussy, gripping and milking his big fat dick and draining it as if her cunt was desperate for his seed. He groaned, working her clit faster, scouring quick circles over it as Jeanette shivered and spasmed over him, her toes arched as her chest heaved, her ample bosoms bouncing directly before his face. Dean Ortiz leaned forward, gnawing and sucking on a nipple as he fucked her through her climax, feeling her hot, tight cunt spout around his big fat cock. He was so near to experience his overwhelming orgasm along with her, yet he held off – he didn't want to come in her cunt. Besides, it would be extremely unpleasant if his new fuck slut got all swollen and stretched with pregnancy, and he didn't let his sluts the luxury of contraception or abortions, regardless of whether he let the entire college football team come up her cunt.

"You truly are a fine slut, aren't you?" he teased, kissing Jeanette's ear as she at last quit shivering and jerking against him.

Jeanette just whimpered accordingly, overwhelmed and conquered by her second climax of the passionate sexual adventure. She could feel his cock pulsating inside her continuously and she cried – "Wouldn't he ever come? Would this ever end?" Her twisted mind screamed her perverted thoughts as she gasped. Her heart pounding like a thousand drums. She was so depleted – her legs felt like jelly, her stomach aching with how hard the Dean had made her orgasm.

Reaching behind her, the Dean extracted the ginger butt plug from her anus. He pulled out of her overflowing pussy, fisting his big fat throbbing cock at the base. The bulbous cock head was messy and shimmering with their blended passionate juices, smooth and glistening with pre-cum, her wetness, and a little blood. He poked the cock head against her little virgin anal cavity, feeling her jerk with sheer shock.

Jeanette's eyes widened. She began to gasp hysterically through her nose, begging behind her gag and shaking her head. She battled against the restraints on her wrists, her chest heaving, and her butt hole clenching.

"What?" the devious Dean inquired, giggling wickedly. "You didn't think I'd fill your pussy, did you? And, knock a gorgeous fuck toy with a baby? I don't think so. Plus, virgin ass is exquisitely tight, and I'm ready to claim that virgin asshole." With that, he grasped her hips, driving his dick into her virgin anal cavity. The ginger had tightened her up, exciting her, stirring her lustful impulses, and it was difficult getting his smooth big fat cock inside her, particularly with her battling him. However, Dean Ortiz was a tenacious man – he pulled her down, forcing her down on his big fat throbbing erection until the ring of her rear end clasped down around the glans. The Dean groaned, curving his hips as Jeanette screamed behind the gag in pain and pleasure. He thrust himself somewhere inside her, overlooking any obstruction; he went on until he was buried deep inside her tight ass. He snorted as it clenched around him.

It felt like a long thick baseball bat was being shoved up her tiny little virgin butt hole. Jeanette shouted and screamed, tears spilling down her reddened cheeks. With the gag in her mouth, her desperate screams were muffled, and nobody came to her help as the wicked Dean rammed his ten-inch big fat cock into her anal cavity. She sobbed and shivered – it burned and ached worse than the hardcore spanking, more terrible than anything she'd felt.

"Who are you? You're my girl...You ache to please me...You beg to serve me...You yearn to worship me...You're my slut, my baby girl, my toy, my property, my love, your body yearns for me, your heart beats for me, your soul longs for my possession, You're mine." The perverse Dean whispered raising goose bumps all over her skin.

"Oh my god, I'm enjoying stretching out your tight little virgin butt-hole," he groaned. It just took only a couple of thrusts of his hips before he shot up inside her butt, shivering and moaning as spurt after spurt of his sensual juices spilled into her reluctant anal cavity. It was so tight, draining him and squeezing him scrumptiously as he emptied his balls. At long last, he was done, and he pulled out with a sigh. Freeing her hands, he pushed her unceremoniously off his lap.

Jeanette snorted as she hit the floor. She tore the gag out of her mouth and cried. She was absolutely depleted, her eyes were red, her ass practically purple from the vicious spanking, bleeding out of both her pussy and her butt hole from the ruthless hardcore fucking that the wicked Dean had given her. What was more awful was that a part of her deviant and perverted mind had delighted in it. She had orgasmed twice from her ordeal, and she was still soaking, her clit still looking out of her pink folds, yearning for more intense pleasure.

"Get dressed and get lost," Dean Ortiz ordered, tucking himself back into his pants. Now that he'd finished with her, he had little enthusiasm for her. "Also, Jeanette? I hope to see you in my office regularly for the rest of the semester. I also think you may require some home mentoring, isn't that right? I've got a collection of exquisite and impeccable hardware that I can hardly wait to acquaint you with."

Sensual Response

My sweetheart was desperate to try anal sex, and so here were...

"Nearly there...?" She said biting her lower lip, squinting in concentration. Audrey is shockingly charming this way. We haven't pushed any number of limits thus far; so this was new for her.

Moreover, the angle wasn't awful. With her head down, ass high up in the air, arms crossed under her cheek and her ankles between my legs, that wonderful lush body arched against me, grinding herself erotically onto my pulsating erection. Her shiny, dark gold hair was disheveled and spread over the delicate skin of her shoulders.

I can feel her gradually unwinding. Being inside her feels amazing; however, this is a distinct sensation. Most thrilling is her response. I can feel the strain from her body; both around my throbbing manhood and the muscles of her back under my massaging fingertips.

This is most intimate. Yet I wondered why I had proposed this. A few scholars experience passionate feelings for the moon and compose poems. I discovered my inspiration in the charming little noises Audrey made with my hard erection almost inside her tight, pink, virgin butthole.

Such charming mewling! She doesn't seem to realize how she's creating them. Those little murmurs begin when she starts to feel more comfortable. Those slight moans and gasps increase when she was courageous enough to thrust further back against me, She emitted little passionate cries when it hurt erotically.

I could experience a mind-blowing orgasm right now, with perhaps a little eye contact blended sensually with the coursing electrifying goosebumps and the perfect combination of salacious whimpers. I'm so achingly hard I could continue fucking her delicious anal hole for ages; simply pound my throbbing erection more profoundly into her arse with the hot natural lubricant coating me.

I held myself still until my eyesight returned, and the conflicting neural cymbals blurred to a lovely static-y throb. I waited until she calmed down and gave me that lust-filled look that says, 'fuck me hard, big man'.

My eyes roamed delicately over her smooth, lush back from where our flesh met and she produced a beautiful sound. Thrillingly, I caught the attention of her blue eyes as she half twisted to gaze back.

"How goes it with you, Gorgeous?" At present, I'm holding still. We've truly been communicating in recent weeks and I'm highly confident that attempting this may be the supreme prize; if we can do it, that is. So far, we're about halfway and Audrey is squirming and groaning like she's being ravished by a steroidal beastly Gorgon. Yet I don't think the energetic beating of my cock inside her lovely anal cavity is making a difference.

"That's no joke…You're too big," Audrey tells me.

"Do you realize what you're saying?" I answer with a chuckle. The insertion is awkward for Audrey and I pull back a bit, to give her some breathing room.

"Moderately big, then…" Audrey doesn't talk in complete sentences when she's being fucked in the ass. We're learning a great deal about one another today.

"Do we need to go to back to the toy for a bit?" I tease and keep any dismay from my voice. I'm in no hurry to end this sensational ecstasy, and Audrey is worth the wait.

"No…" She mumbles and begins thrusting back onto my cock. The friction is sweet for me. However, I realize that more lube would make things erotically easier.

"Fuck…" I guess I match my action to my words when I'm extremely horny, or describe what I'm doing, it depends on how you look at it. "Audrey…" I snarl and tumble to rest over her back with my weight on my knuckles, my hands on either side of hers.

"I love you." She moaned, relaxing somewhat as she spoke the words.

"I love you too," I replied, tensing up a bit. Christ, this was extraordinary. This felt like a virginity she'd been hiding all this time, and I was the lucky bastard to find it and to pop her cherry.

I realized this would be a bizarre time to propose, and that I would need to make up an anecdote about where I was when I determined that Audrey was the one for me, assuming we had a story we could tell in polite company.

I understood I needed a ring as well. Custom truly slowed my impulses every now and then.

Audrey thrusted farther than before; she felt my thighs colliding with hers and we tensed together.

"Easy..." I snorted at the extraordinary sensation of being wrapped by her. However, as magnificent as it felt for me; I needed to remember that this was Audrey's first time.

"Oww..." She cried delicately, making an effort not to withdraw from the sting. I pull back again gradually.

"Here, lie down further," I state. "Is it terrible?"

"I've had greater pains than this." Audrey was so adorable when she was under-representing her discomfort. We shared a laugh.

I gradually pulled my still pulsating cock out of her. Audrey recoiled as I popped out of her and lay relaxing on the bed.

She hurried a bit, figuring she could simply thrust back against me and relax after, not before. That sort of wild fuck appears to be somewhat exceptional for a first attempt.

My passionate kisses leave little smears of dampness on her lush skin, gleaming in the light as I cuddle between her thighs to give her smooth, hot, burning pussy some sensual consideration.

She was soaking wet, swollen, and sticky. As if we'd been out the whole day and I'd been showering her with sensual kisses and exquisite touches until she was nearly humping my leg, and she was unable to take care of erotic business until we got back to the car...

Good times! I regularly wound up remembering things like that while devouring my golden darling's pink slit.

"Mmm..." Audrey gave out a low, expressive groan again. Despite the fact that she's a little sore she's still as horny as I am. Nobody said anything about ending the erotic and sensual rendezvous.

Spreading out her arms, Audrey focused on the coziness of the bed underneath her. When my lips delicately pull at her clit, she spread out her legs to give me better access.

"You're so possessed by my pussy..." She prods me in a languid, distracted voice. I answer with an uproarious sucking commotion as I lick and kiss her clit, making her shudder and then laugh.

To be honest, I was obsessed with her butt and her juicy tits as well. Audrey had an expansive appeal, not only due to her slim, agile body. When I found myself watching her sleeping in my arms, I couldn't get enough of the gorgeousness she possessed. I enjoyed just hearing her breathing. I'd never acknowledged I was so emotional.

I was going to become mixed up in a joyous little dream while I sucked her sacred hole, yet Audrey supportively squirmed her butt under my palms holding herself open to me. I sometimes thought we should have attempted this many months before if I didn't continue getting to taste her, overlooking everything else.

This wasn't exactly what she was asking me to do. However, I let out a low snarl of joy as I continued licking and kissing gradually moving upward from her pussy to her rear end.

"Oh... God..." She snickers in the middle of the words shocked at my intensity. I've never kissed her there; she'd been too bashful to even think about letting me do this.

However, she was letting me now, and the groan that interrupted her chuckling was tempting enough for me to continue. She tasted of the gel we'd been generously applying, cherry-flavored. Cherry gel for popping her anal virginity was how I figured.

"Fuck..." Audrey's voice is shamelessly loud for a second and then she quiets herself down, becoming flushed from head to toe as she places the back of her hand over her lips.

I had my mouth full, so I just snarled between the dazzling folds of her rear and tenderly slide my warm tongue inside her.

"Oh my God..." Audrey is truly exceeding herself with the erotic commentary today. It's the major reason why I've been unshakable, extremely aroused, and overly excited for the past couple of hours, and simply like Audrey, I'm beginning to get a little throb of anticipation somewhere deep inside.

Audrey squirms slightly on the bed. This new thrilling sensation is likely where we ought to have begun. Yet, the build-up is significant; she would've been too bashful to even think about letting me do this without a ton of sensational foreplay, snuggling and an uncommon transitory bringing down her inhibitions.

She feels nearly as tight to my tongue, yet as I reach beneath my mouth to rub her clit with the pad of my thumb, she loosens up her butt.

"Mmm." I mutter, not ceasing. We're gaining ground.

"Like..." Audrey trails off. "Like that?" I could see the bright pink blush wash over her radiant skin, and the constrained yet sensual bit of her rear end and back that I could see.

"Mhmm..." I murmured once more, with passion. Audrey appeared to have gotten the hang of loosening up; allowing me to give her long licks just as tenderly fucking her with my warm, moist tongue.

Audrey tensed up, her feet had been making sluggish circles yet now her legs straightened and wrapped tightly around me.

"Ooh..." Audrey was lying with her head on her crossed arms, her eyes closed as she concentrated on the incredible feeling.

For a moment, I wondered whether Audrey had orgasmed before I expected, it was a nearly done deal and even she wasn't certain from the start. She braced her thighs hard on either side of my neck, and attempted to wring the last exciting and wonderful sensation from her animated nerves.

I attempted to shove my tongue as deep into her as I could. I've had something of an oral obsession. However, in Audrey's case my enthusiasm was a direct result of the manner in which she responded.

"Fuck me..." Audrey said in a whine. I grinned and continued with my prodding licks, laughing slightly.

"No, truly," Audrey said in a more desperate tone. "I'm ready. Fuck me..." She groaned once more as I circled her butt with the tip of my tongue, plunging in to prod her once more.

I was truly hungry for it by then, I scooped my arm under her hips and lifted her up to her knees. She gazed at me, the sight along her arching back as I spread gel onto her, and then onto myself.

"Mmm..." She murmured for me as I pressed the tip of my cock into her anal cavity once more. It was easier this time. Audrey drew a hand between her legs to caress her clit simultaneously.

"Perfect..." I was going to say something different. However, I simply trailed off into a delightfully passionate little moan at the warm, exquisite, smooth feeling of her.

I watched her eyes as we returned to about where we'd been before. She nibbled her lip and watched me.

I thrust in, gradually, firmly, and Audrey backed into me a little as we collided in the middle. Following half a month of erotic and brainstorming discussions and a couple of fun-loving endeavors with fingers and toys, we were finally there!

"Oh..." Audrey made such a delicate, intimate, little and passionate moan. It wasn't uproarious before however it felt like the entire house had gone quiet. I was helped to remember other sensual moments with her. It felt like the first time we kissed.

I paused for a minute and watched her glowing face as I ran comforting palms over her lush, radiant back. Her eyes were shut now. However, she gave me a slight nod, moaning against the pillows.

I pulled out almost my entire length and gradually shoved back in, evoking another low erotic moan from both of us. It was moronic to play favorites with Audrey's body, yet this was extraordinary. This sort of closeness was new to the two of us; it added an anxious vitality to each tremendous sensation. It wasn't simply sex when you were exploring this way.

I continued with the moderate fuck and got a similar moderate flex from Audrey as she moved on the bed and adjusted me up perfectly.

It'd been a moment since I'd spoken to her, I noticed.

"Having a fabulous time, Gorgeous?" Her eyes opened and she reddened a profound crimson red, gnawed her lip once more. I loved when she did that.

I reiterated the question with a moderate, profound thrust, a simple cadence I could have kept up the whole day.

"Mmm..." Audrey turned her head to lie on the opposite side, staying away from my watchful eye yet at the same time pushing back against my cock.

"That is a 'yes'." I leaned down and adjusted my weight with one hand, holding myself somewhere inside her as we changed position. Presently Audrey's perfectly arched back was squeezed to my chest, my arms snaked underneath her hips to bring her as tight against me as I could.

"Fuck..." I murmured in her ear, and kissed her cheek as she laughed. I acted all cool and reserved. I recalled that Audrey was stripped and we were fucking. Regardless of how often we did it, the idea never got old.

I skimmed my hands up her body and grabbed hold of her succulent bosoms as I pummeled deeper into her butt. The two of us were lost in the sensations for some time. That moderate fuck was like a dirty, erotic dance, neither of us felt any urge to do anything other than relish one another.

"I love you." I licked her earlobe after I said it. I let out a long moan as she took me in completely now.

"I love you too, dear." She chuckled. I felt the sensational vibration of it inside her.

"What's funny?" I whispered in her ear, incapable of giving a lot of thought to anything besides holding her and penetrating her as if conquering her soul.

"You go all warm and fluffy when you fuck me." Audrey chuckled once more, and then groaned as I flexed my cock deep inside her soft anal cavity.

"Warm and fluffy?" I attempted to pass on what I thought about this in the more assertive thrust, the lively crush of her nipples between my fingers and thumbs.

Audrey didn't respond for a couple of seconds. I reminded myself that this was a first for her. Audrey lethargically lifted her head and turned the other way to confront me.

"Mmm..." Audrey stirs under me. "You're so genuine until you're fucking me, then you..." She trailed off as extraordinary sensations coursed through her.

"Then what?" I thrust harder, prodding her once more.

"Ahh..." Audrey reached behind her to grasp the back of my neck by the hair, pressing me tight. I kissed the nape of her neck and tugged her juicy bosoms in my grasp, waiting impatiently for her answer.

She reddened and was distracted, her pouty lips gaped slightly as she inhaled deeper and faster, getting almost breathless, battling to adjust until I put a steady arm around her.

What the heck, we can talk later.

I kissed between her shoulder-blades, making her shudder. I put one hand there to hold her head down as I began fucking her harder and quicker.

I figured Audrey might very well be a natural. This new electrifying sensation made her writhe and squirm as she did when I moved her clit between my lips.

The extraordinary thing about her was that she was full of surprises. I hadn't realized that she could draw until we'd been dating for four months. Now I had one of her drawings inked on my arm. This time she astounded me by getting so into it she got nearly... serious.

Audrey, step by step, balanced up onto her elbows and I lifted up to give her room. One arm balanced us while the other was still wrapped lovingly around her chest.

She lifted up further and we both wobbled for a second as we changed from inclined to some minor variation from doggy, and now into an erotically moderate kind of pound in my lap as I knelt and she curved her back.

I needed to say something. I was too keen to even think about interrupting this passionately wanton state of mind she was in. Things were great when Audrey was feeling courageous and explorative.

"You fucker..." She blamed me lovingly, as though this was certifiably not a joint exercise, as though it wasn't her grinding down onto my cock that was causing her to feel that way.

I stayed silent, tolerating the approval along with the blame. I bit her earlobe in that friendly 'you're mine' kind of way.

Typically that made her chuckle. Sometimes it made her so sensitive she would fend me off. Today, she moaned low and noisy, impatiently waiting for me to do her. I felt the incredible, exciting vibration of it in her chest, and afterward, she lifted her hands off the bed and wrapped them over my shoulders.

Riding in my lap, curving her back, sticking her chest out as I returned to holding her abundant bosoms in each hand; maneuvering her down onto me somewhat harder as Audrey truly began getting into the mood.

"... fuckin' love you..." I state between moans as I embraced her more tightly to my chest, passionately, never willing to let her go; always desperate to freeze the moment with her this way.

"... love you..." Audrey never neglected to react to those three dirty words. It turned into an erotic game for me to state it when she was losing herself.

She was panting breathlessly, gasping and holding my neck and shoulders hard. I tugged her nipples just to make her groan and afterward folded my arms over her hips so I could fuck her harder.

"... fucker..." She was still calling me names, and I wanted to even the score.

"… you're the…" I attempted; however, Audrey had begun exploring different avenues of thrusting me as she rode me, and it took a moment for me to concentrate on what she was doing.

"You were… saying?" She chuckled, grinding down further into my lap. I realized that she had assumed control over the last couple of minutes. The lady was tricky. I loved that.

I moaned and abandoned the exchange of dialogue. We could think later.

She felt great; smooth and flexible, gleaming with perspiration, burning like a bitch in heat. Never, under any circumstance, did I need to release her. So I hung tight, gritted my teeth, kissed the back of her neck, and snarled the way that made her shudder.

With a few more enthusiastic thrusts, Audrey came at the same time I did. It was difficult to tell who'd set who off. I figured it was her charming groans and the guileful look in her eyes.

Warmth crawled under my skin, and I felt the coolness of her shoulder against my cheek as I embraced her, easing back down however not halting.

Audrey felt it for a wild electrifying second, an erotic blend of min/maxed vibes that caused the orgasm to appear to be unmanageable. She tensed hard around me, held herself still on my lap and let out a loud low moan.

"Fucking…" Audrey now and then showcases her actions to words. Yet this time, she lets out a shivery sort of moan that pulls the last of my climax from my body.

Audrey, being a hotshot on a basic level, figured out how to prop herself up and I don't have the foggiest idea why. I need to stay still for a moment I was excessively overwhelmed by Audrey's power.

"Mmm…" A charming little whine escaped her throat halfway as she figured out how to get in one full breath. She was shivering in my lap, weak as her hands descended to grasp my thighs under her for help.

I laughed, rubbed my cheek against hers and embraced her tightly as she unwound into my arms in stages.

We wobble as she ignored the need to adjust her balance, yet I was prepared for it. I kept her steady, and heard her delightful laughter as she recalled what we'd just done.

"Mhmm…" She agrres with something one of us had said, making me chuckle.

My chuckle made my cock throb inside her and she groaned, flexing her back against my chest.

"That was…" I was at a loss for words.

"Yeah…" She agreed with me.

With a couple of lust-filled moans, we parted, and she turned over in the bed.

I watched my reflection in her eyes, considering that we'd just had our first time together like that, that it went so well, and that we might consider a second time.

"You're really amazing, Babe," I confessed to her. I've said this before. However she appeared to believe me this time. It would've been worth the wait just for that.

"Well, then you're the second best." She teased me.

We kissed.

Wild Discretion – Part 1

It was another assignment, another business trip out of town and the usual level of travel chaos for Frank Mayhem. The standard routine procedure included booking flights, hotels, and transfers to arrange. However, this time, all appeared to go quite smoothly. Instead of getting his secretary to arrange every minute travel details for him, where he wound up in exotic and luxury hotels, Frank decided to try something much less fashionable and lavish. This time, Frank preferred to be surrounded by fewer people in business suits that always filled the rooms of the usual hotels he where he stayed.

Frank's business trips allowed him the luxury of a few down days, a little reward he thought. So he chose to organize his own accommodation in a small, yet elegant and classy boutique-style hotel, on the outskirts of Atlanta, far away from the hustle and bustle of the city life. Something simple, unembellished, just the sort of place where he surely wouldn't come across anyone in suits. It was the type of peaceful accommodation where he could chillax in and could delight himself with a couple of easy slow hours forgetting the exhausting sales targets in the world of corporate insurance.

Opening the door to his room, Frank was thrilled to find it adequately furnished and decorated yet refined, and it was creatively different compared to the type of hotels he typically stayed at. It consisted of the basic pieces: a simple wooden bed covered with a lovely white cotton bedspread and other necessary furniture all within whitewashed walls. It was reminiscent of the Greek style interior. Accompanying it was a delightfully enchanting balcony overlooking the crystal clear, aqua-toned pool below. It was all Frank craved for before flying back. It was an excellent accommodation offering a perfect couple of days of relaxation to escape from his boring routine life's hustle.

Feeling more relaxed, Frank ventured into the bar and the elegant restaurant that extended around one side of the pool. Settling himself down, Frank ordered a beer and curiously looked about watching the world around him. It seemed, by all accounts, to be a classic family-run restaurant with the inclusion of a few additional stewards and waitresses, generally youngsters in their mid 20's, or so Frank presumed. The hiring of the additional staffs was likely done for the busier periods.

A couple of beers later and Frank was absolutely enjoying the vibe of the place. Sitting alone, he appreciated the life moving around him. However, he felt that the majority of customers weren't just lodgers. Most of them were there to simply relish the delights of the restaurant's tasty cuisines.

What Frank did notice after his third beer was that another young lady had joined the shift, perhaps, for the busier evening and night trade. His eyes continued catching her tempting curves as she moved back and forth between the bar and café, taking a growing number of orders that were increasingly mounting as the day ended.

Frank strove hard not to stare at her. He certainly didn't want to present himself as the single lurking predator ogling the young and attractive waitresses in the restaurant. But he couldn't help it. He was most intrigued by her presence. She was distinctive in a manner Frank was trying to figure out in his mind and she stood out from the rest of the staff.

She was not an incredible marvel in the perfect sense of the word, though she had a delightfully raw seduction that Frank continued to be attracted to. He could see she had striking dark eyes that looked alive. Perhaps, those eyes had secrets buried in them deeper and darker than the mysterious seas, he thought. Her brown hair resembled the continuous waves of a waterfall, falling a little savagely to her shoulders.

She had tempting curves, even in her somewhat used and over-washed hotel outfit. The buttons of her top just managed to hold together the thin cotton fabric encasing what Frank could see were perky ample bosoms. In fact, when she brought over his fourth beer, Frank couldn't help but observe the oozing eroticism as she leaned somewhat over his table. The edges of her blouse slightly separated revealing the shapely full skin of her breasts underneath. The sight was so hypnotic that it captivated every sense and function of his body. "God, they looked hot," Frank tried to calm his wild excitements. The sight of her cleavage was feeding his unbridled lust. There was a moment when Frank finally understood that he needed to stop staring at her. But, when he caught her studying his looks, he felt as if she had such a cheerful soul. Perhaps, she didn't have any concerns whatsoever with him staring just a little too much.

"Would you like something with your beer?" She asked with a brilliant smile while bringing down her chest significantly closer to his eye line. Her voice was so exotic that it intoxicated him. Within seconds, his mind was in absolute chaos playing the lyrics of his heart.

"Oh, thank you. No, this is just perfect. Thank you!" Frank faltered a little. The girl understood the reason and she giggled even more. That alluring curve of her face, that damn smile made his heart skip a beat as he fumbled for words. He was in trouble, mayhem actually.

"Well, in case you need anything, feel free to ask if I can interest you in anything else from the bar or the restaurant," and with that remark, she moved away leaving Frank wondering what else this waitress could interest him in.

He spent the rest of the evening at the bar, and downed a few more beers and ate chicken paprika served on a bed of blended rice with a form of delectable roasted salad. The meal was simple, exquisite and superbly exceptional much like the rooms. As the evening progressed, Frank cherished the chilled vibes and the relaxing atmosphere and obviously, getting the odd stray expressions from his fun-loving distraction, her playful eyes, and revealing blouse as the waitress served his table. Of course, she had caught him off-guard and thrown him off balance. And, she loved his attention as much as she enjoyed having an advantage.

Undoubtedly, there was a carefree energetic soul which she exuded in her non-verbal expressions, adding a crude attraction to her attitude. To him, she was a reckless wanderer, so gorgeous, so beautiful that she could light up the world with her friendly smile.

His heart pounded like bass drums. He felt it was about to jump out of his chest. As he continued gazing her, he felt like the predator and the prey, the conqueror and the conquered, though unsure of what he truly was. Moreover, Frank thought the alluring woman realized that and she sensed the intense temptation she was creating within him. Perhaps, Frank was too immature to hide his feelings effectively regardless of his desperate attempts to do so. As an attractive provocatrix, she made it impossible and too exciting for him not to be captivated by her presence.

As she moved about, Frank discovered her occasionally and overtly brushing by his table, just a little close not to seem intentional.

"What is her goal? Was she sending him signals?" Frank wondered as he glanced from the corner of his eye at the temptress for the rest of the evening. Other than to guarantee he couldn't take his attention off her as her shift progressed, perhaps that was the interest the waitress meant to evoke. With that enthusiastic interest from such an ardent admirer, she absolutely seemed, by all accounts, to be getting excited too.

How time and the evening passed, Frank was absolutely clueless. Soon her shift was over and Frank found the bar clearing of customers and staff. He stood and headed back to his room.

When he'd stepped out of the bar, he heard a seductive voice say: "Hey there, did you enjoy your time in there?" As soon as he turned around, he spotted Janice Jayne unwinding on a couch beside the entrance of the bar facing the pool reading a book. Frank was baffled and before he could respond to her, she teased again, "She seemed to be quite interested in you."

Fumbling for words while gathering his composure, he responded, "Goodness, Janice! How're you? How come I didn't notice you before now?"

"I feel marvelous, thanks. By the way, I had no intention of disturbing you while you were so busy focusing on your distraction," Janice teased with another smile.

All Frank could do was blush and laugh to acknowledge what she'd said. While Janice spoke, she never looked up, but stayed focused on the pages of her book and was clearly oblivious to her surroundings. Yet, her investigating eyes never missed the actions of her small-town neighborhood boy.

Frank was fortunate she was focused on her reading since she possessed a hungry look in her eyes and it frightened him. Whenever his innocent eyes focused in on that sort of scene, it never failed to stir a stimulating response in him. Curled up on the sofa, wearing an oversized, navy blue robe, eyes glued to the pages of a mystery novel and holding a cigarette, Janice could inhale Frank's heart, and exhale his soul. She could just smoke him out.

If the mysteriously attractive waitress was his distraction for the entire evening, Janice could invariably be the woman corrupting his mind without ever knowing what she was doing. The smoke of her Sobranie changed colors as it ascended past the lampshade while curling up from her hand that relaxed on the arm of the sofa.

Frank knew Janice had started smoking at around 15. Something about getting a hard-on each time she lit up enlightened him. Janice was almost ten years older than Frank. She was in her late thirties. Frank knew the fascination he had was somewhat outside the 'standard' and should be kept private. Yet, beyond any doubt he couldn't resist the temptation to sneak looks whenever he saw she wasn't looking.

This was before the Internet. Certainly, Frank didn't enjoy the unlimited access to an endless stream of pornography of any kind that was accessible today. So those psychological photos made a difference. Frank knew from his late teens that Janice was into writing. However, he never heard of any published or acclaimed works of hers.

Her smoking style was mindfully relaxed and simple yet with the manner in which she played out a small cheek-pop before a brisk snap after each drag before breathing in deeply and executing a tight, one breath out, she generally passed on specific decadence and blissful fulfillment. It was easy to see that she loved smoking and took her time to appropriately relish it.

While Frank never believed Janice was smoking for him when he would steal glances, those moments felt very private. Frank would try to discover ways to associate with her so when she smoked, he could watch without being too obvious. There were many evenings where the two of them would watch TV shows or a movie where Frank would really get his own 'private screening.'

"So, back to your room now?" Janice asked.

"Guess so. I've got a meeting to attend tomorrow morning." Frank seemed pitiful about his condition. If he hadn't been burdened with sales targets he would never dare to deny his stimulating interactions with Janice.

"Would you mind having a drink with me in my room? I promise not to keep you awake for long." Janice teased again. The glimmer in her eyes was too provocative to reject. All Frank could do was smile and nod his acknowledgment.

As soon as the pair reached her room, Janice moved to the cozy couch in a relatively dark corner of her room. With a single lamp lighting the table, the environment felt warm which made everything look more pleasant. Relaxing comfortably on the couch opposite, Frank selected a bottle of French burgundy and Garbure soup from the menu before dialing the reception to place the order. By the time their food arrived, they had already toasted to their fantastic evening and almost polished off the bottle. Moreover, the intoxicating effect of the alcohol greased their conversation which gradually turned more personal.

As time progressed, Frank was welcomed with the exquisitely sensual images of Janice's long legs. The lights in the room were off, except for the low reading light behind the beige couch where she sat. The smoke from her full lips took on a pale blue shade as she exhaled. She was wearing a cotton robe. Her reading glasses were low on her nose and appeared to be captivated by the book she was reading.

Watching Janice in this private moment, Frank immediately felt his erection start to harden and he needed to repress the overpowering longing to rub the palm of his hand against its hardness. Fortunately, he was wearing a long shirt that masked the rapidly developing tent in his trousers. However, it didn't prevent him from ensuring it was pulled as low as possible under those tempting circumstances. Chilling with Janice, along with a couple of drinks and tremendous arousal, in the late evening had "unbalanced" written all over it.

"Happy to be back?" Janice asked which again started them on a discussion about his personal life. Janice took the opportunity to casually ask Frank if he was dating anyone.

Frank averted the question and answered calmly: "There is no one special. I just meet a few girls now and then". Frank got some information about her work and interests and while she was courteous in her replies, Frank sensed there was a boredom developing.

Janice was divorced and now was absolutely committed to her writing and the main excitement it appeared she was getting was from her mystery books. The only time she appeared to get amped up for something was when Frank asked her what she was reading.

"So, what are you reading with such fascination?" Frank asked.

"Oh, nothing. It's just some writer named Annie J Mar. I'm actually proofreading it before I send it to the publishers." Janice smiled.

"Annie J Mar! Seriously! I'm such a big fan of hers! Her novels are so erotic and always have such unimaginable twists and turns." Frank enthused.

Janice raised her eyebrows. Certainly, she never hoped to have an ardent follower of novels that evening. Now, to Frank's excitement, the story was turning out to be a whole new one. It was working with each long moderate drag Janice took off her cigarette. Perpetually, those drags would come amidst Frank's reminiscence of some tale from his teen years. It required him to concentrate on what he was thinking of and not what he was staring at. Frank always preferred this piece of his Janice fantasy.

From where Frank was sitting, and the angle of the couch, Frank had the exquisite pleasure to subtly observe the profile of Janice's face without her, seeing him. She tapped a Sobranie out of the pack, reached for her lighter and delicately placed the cigarette in her mouth in a sultry manner, tempting Frank's stimulating fantasies in an especially sensational way. She simply gave the cigarette a chance to dangle there, the lighter just inches away waiting patiently to be lit; yet her absolute fixation was on the book she was reading.

His erection became more evident with every passing minute. Frank was still high and the fantasy-like state just enabled him to fall further into the profundities of his fantasy. Mercifully, Janice fired up the lighter and, never taking her eyes off the page, moved it to the tip of her Sobranie, crumbled her cheeks with a hard drag, breathed in without expelling it from her tightened lips and gradually put the lighter back down on the table. The first blast of smoke arrived in a surge out of her nose as she once again dragged hard, popped her cheeks a bit in her own style, held the smoke in her mouth before executing an ideal quick snap, breathed in deeply again before breathing out a long, slender stream of smoke that moved over the book.

Frank's cock was as big and full and hard as he'd never felt it before.

Frank sat like that unobtrusively and viewed every action of his fantasy queen as she smoked her cigarette. He tried desperately not to focus so hard on her. However, he continued sneaking looks at Janice. It felt perverse this time. Possibly it was because he was meeting her after such a long time and as a grown man. However, his eyes were devouring the sight of an alluring, smoking hot, temptress he used to stroke his shaft to in his youthful fantasies and increasingly like the attractive smoking lady he always craved to kiss.

"You know, I never asked you this," Janice said. "But, do you ever smoke?"

Like many individuals who appreciate the picture of smoking, Frank smoked, but not often. His smoking was saved for special events like being drunk or high, which he certainly qualified for right now, or when he was extremely aroused and stimulated while stroking off. What's more, since Janice's inquiry was more of an invitation than curiosity, and the thrilling idea of offering something as intimate as smoking with her, set his testosterone levels into high gear. There was no chance he was going to turn down the offer.

"I smoke once-in-a-while; after I've had a couple of drinks," Frank replied with a little embarrassment and shyness in his voice. After all, she was still quite a bit older for the love of all that is holy. She knew him when he was 12 and he felt that he was doing something "terrible" by admitting to her that he, at times, smoked.

"Well, I know you've had a couple of drinks. So what do you say? Is this a "once-in-a-while" Mr. Mayhem," Janice teasingly asked as she tapped out a Sobranie from the packet and held it between two fingers in an offering gesture. "Oh good," Janice teased. "Franky is going to smoke for me. I simply love a man who smokes," and with that, she gave him first a Sobranie and then the lighter.

Now, not only was Frank feeling an overwhelming surge of accomplishing something as "grown-up" as smoking with a more seasoned lady but he was doing it with the woman he had always fantasized about in his erotic dreams. As Janice carried the fire to his cigarette, Frank rehashed her activities from before and delicately guided her hand to the end of his cigarette.

In the wake of taking a hard drag, battling the short desperation to cough out the smoke, and feeling thrilled by the surge of nicotine filling his nerves and changed mental state, Frank breathed out with an audible 'ahhh.'

"Feels better, doesn't it?" Janice chuckled as she took the still flaming lighter and lit her own. She also took a long drag and made a bit of an 'ahhh' as she exhaled too which caused them both to giggle.

"It's wonderful to feel incredibly great, isn't it?" Janice asked.

She didn't know the half of it.

"Indeed it is. I always try to continue 'feeling incredibly great' on my schedule," Frank replied before his own super-pleasurable exhale.

Janice empowered Frank by grinning and offering a "That is the best way to do it," before giving his leg a pat and repositioning herself on the sofa to turn directly towards him, abandoning any pretense of reading her novel any further.

"Do you want to know the biggest reason why I began to smoke," she said wickedly. "I was about seventeen and my first boyfriend used to tell me he thought that young ladies looked extremely provocative when they smoked. Besides, he always used to say: 'A good smoker, like a good lover, always takes his time with a cigar.'"

"My God, really?" Frank reacted as calmly as possible, trying to hide his growing excitement.

"What's more, you may not know this, but 18-year-old young ladies truly need boys to believe they're provocative, sassy and classy" she stated, thinking back with a seductive grin.

"So he was your motivation for smoking," Frank asked, desperately hoping she would continue down this line of reasoning.

"No doubt," Janice stated, taking a profound, cheek-hollowing drag before inhaling the smoke into her lungs for the nicotine jolt and rapidly blowing a long steady flow into the air. "I'll accuse him," she said laughing. "We used to get a kick out of going up to Flat Top...you've likely been up there on more than one occasion, right?" Janice asked teasingly.

Frank certainly didn't like to tell her that he'd been up there several times getting unbelievably stoned with his friends. So he simply off-handedly said, "Yeah, you know, teenage rush, once or twice." Janice chuckled a bit. "All things considered, I'm sure you realized what happens up there," she said as though we shared a secret.

"So he made you smoke up at Flat Top," Frank asked, endeavoring to lure her back towards the subject he expected to hear most about. "Is that what you'd do up there?"

Janice chuckled mischievously, "As well as other things, yes. But no doubt, that's where he made me smoke." She paused for a moment to take another drag of her now half-smoked Sobranie. Frank did the same, mimicking the length of her inhale so that they each exhaled together; their smoke meeting and blending perfectly in the air crafting a kind of smoky communion.

Frank was sure the mature lady's peering eyes never missed that delightful sight.

"I remember that we were discussing how my best friend Pauline had started smoking. She inquired as to whether I'd ever want to smoke. I had an Aunt that smoked and I'd constantly sort of liked being around it. I snuck a Sobranie from her case when I was around 14 years old. I went into the washroom when she wasn't anywhere nearby and watched myself in the mirror. Wow! That was so blissful!" Janice chuckled mischievously as she exhaled her puff of smoke.

"I did that too when I smoked for the very first time," Frank blurted out too rapidly. That wasn't a touch of maturity in his character. Certainly, he should be more careful than blurting this out. Janice raised her eyebrows and paused with an inquiring look on her face.

"I mean," Frank clarified with somewhat less vitality. "I sort of watched myself as well. Just to see what it looks like, you know?"

"Did you cough your lungs up as well?" Janice asked and they both laughed at the shared memory of their first cigarettes.

Janice continued with her story. "So when my boyfriend asked whether I'd ever smoked, I told him that story. I remember how embarrassed he was when he told me he thought young ladies who smoked were attractive. Ah! He was a shy guy! When I told him, I'd like to try and smoke for him he was super excited. However, we didn't have any cigarettes!"

"Ha!" Frank laughed, somewhat boisterously.

"So, whenever we went up to Flat Top he always came prepared," Janice stated, taking one final hard drag and efficiently crushing out the cigarette in the ashtray.

"All I truly remember about the smoking part was that it wasn't as awful as I suspected it would be," she said. "Yet, I definitely remember what it did to him," she continued, insinuating the way that it clearly stimulated and fascinated her boyfriend. At that point, Janice changed gears. "Hey, I hope you don't mind me telling you all this. I haven't thought about any of this for years. Maybe it's the wine talking," Janice stated almost apologetically.

"Are you kidding me," Frank said enthusiastically. "I love hearing stuff like this. So... after your first successful smoking attempt, you began to smoke more?"

"I did," Janice answered going after yet another Sobranie. "See what happens when I talk about smoking? I already need another," and then she carried the cigarette to her mouth for her temptingly well-practiced and intensely erotic light up and drag.

With the smoke still in her lungs, Janice stated, "So...", before breathing out a huge thick plume of smoke up in the air and over his head and proceeding with, "I figured with his getting a kick out of the chance to watch me and how it made me look and feel, I got into it pretty quickly."

They both were quiet for a couple of minutes. She took another drag and then stated, "You can have another one if you need."

Frank was desperate for another. His irresistible desire to smoke with the woman of his fantasies was too intriguingly captivating to resist. Besides, Frank too had a taste for a special breed of woman. Given the choice between a woman and a cigar...he always preferred the woman with a cigar. Moreover, his stomach ached with the overwhelming urge to reveal to her how hot she was, the manner by which he'd jacked off to her dreaming about her smoking and how irresistibly attractive she was with that lightening stick between her luscious lips.

Instead, Frank said, "You'll get me hooked," and reach for the Sobranies on the coffee table and took a cigarette. He didn't see the lighter. Janice saw it resting on her lap. But instead of passing it over to him, she lit it and held it up.

"Here you go," she asserted in a voice that was both throaty and friendly. Their faces were exceptionally close.

"Thank you," Frank said, leaning toward the fire acknowledging her thoughtfulness.

She put out the flame with a flick of her fingers, dropped the lighter on her lap, took a long sip from her drink and an equally long drag off her cigarette. The commitment Janice exhibited for each drag attracted Frank like a moth to a flame. Frank had to turn away, avert his gaze which was threatening to transform into a leer.

"I guess everybody has a reason behind taking up smoking, huh?" she inquired. "A few people want to show themselves as grown-ups. Perhaps, a few people have always been around it and it's no big deal. For me, it was because I had a boyfriend who got of thrill out of watching me.

When I went to college, well, I had a number of friends who were into almost everything. Cigars, weed, drugs...and I often used to skip classes with my friends just to relish the blissful moments of fire and smoke." Janice paused for a second and after that in a quieter, practically bashful tone stated, "And I guess I got a kick out of the chance to be watched."

For a moment, Frank felt as if he was talking with a young woman his own age. There was still maturity in her ways; however, her tone was that of a more youthful alluring temptress. "She definitely has witchcraft in those luscious lips." Frank thought unwittingly. And the next moment, she was admitting a secret to a trusted friend.

"And, you know what?" Janice's voice was stern.

"What?" Frank mumbled.

"Can I trust you as a friend? Just between us?" Never in the entire discussion, had she seemed so serious.

"Absolutely," Frank was enthusiastic, excited at the possibility that she thought of him as "a friend."

"You like watching me smoke too, don't you?" Janice was smiling mischievously.

She said it unassumingly. It was more a statement than a serious question. Her brilliant eyes were locked on his. She was scanning every facet and nuance of his soul. Or perhaps, that's what crossed his mind as he gazed at his reflection in her sparkling eyes. Frank didn't have the faintest idea what to say.

With a soothing voice perfectly blended with a protective and a seductive temptation, she leaned back and rested her hand at the back of her head.

"It's alright. I get it."

Still absolutely focused on his eyes, she carried the Sobranie to her mouth. She hollowed her cheeks on the long draw, gave an unpretentious yet impeccable snap and with the smoke still in her lungs stated, "You don't fool me. I have seen you watching me, you know?"

Then, when the final word left her mouth, she gradually, drowsily breathed out just to the side of his face, her lips pressed together and her aim was intentional. She didn't smoke for the fake highs that nicotine gave to its inhalers. She always smoked to give her body a perfect excuse to release her from the wretched cage that was trying to hold her down. She smoked because she knew that the Gods if they existed at all weren't interested in her free-spirited soul. She smoked because she loved flirting with death than the arranged marriage with life. She was so insanely wild.

"In fact, to tell you the truth, and remember this is between us, OK? I think I like it." The wicked grin on her face, the luscious lips uttering witchcraft and the plume of smoke liberating wild seduction was enough to proclaim, "Oh darling, you really have no idea who you're dealing with... Do you?

Her body was facing him. Frank had his feet on the ground, his shirt pulled as low as possible over the exceptionally hard erection that was pushing so hard against his trousers it was getting to be agonizing. Frank didn't move. Or perhaps, he had no strength to move. He was absolutely hypnotized by her tempting looks and rich voice drumming through his ears as goosebumps over coursed his skin.

"Yeah?" Frank asked delicately.

"Yeah," Janice said. "You do as well? Do you like to watch me smoke?" And with that, she took a hard drag, sucked it deep inside her lungs and without moving her hand far from her mouth, hit the cigarette similarly that hard. Janice held it in for one minute and after that, gradually, slowly, ever so slowly breathed out past his face, yet closer this time. So close.

"Yes," Frank enthusiastically admitted. "I like to watch you smoke."

Saying so out loud to somebody out of the blue that he found smoking appealing was really something. But saying it to the woman who had excited and stimulated his smoking fantasy meant pushing the limits for Frank Mayhem.

Janice looked at him for a moment and after that with equal amounts of interest and playfulness stated, "I wonder whether you'd like what my boyfriend used to like?" She gestured for

Frank to come towards her with the hand that held the cigarette between her little sexy fingers. "Come here," she said.

As Frank obediently, and nervously, leaned in towards her, Janice took another cheek-emptying, power drag only this time she did an amazingly slow to open mouth inhale; the smoke drifting gradually past her opened lips before she snapped it rapidly into her lungs. Then she murmured, "Close your eyes." Frank did as he was told.

After a moment, Frank felt what must be depicted as the most intoxicating smell he'd ever experienced. He felt the coolness of her breath and tasted the sweetness of her smoke as she tenderly covered his face with her exhale. He'd never smelled anything like it. It was oozing with raw temptation. It reeked of sex. Frank felt his heart beat quicken. He licked his parched lips nervously.

"Oh, wow," Frank exclaimed. A greater number of words were unnecessary.

"Ahhh...so you like that as well, huh?" A mischievous grin spread over her face at her thrilling discovery.

"Yeah....that was wild."

"It was, wasn't it?" she stated, letting Frank know that this blissful joy wasn't a one-sided affair. She gazed at him for two or three seconds as though she were settling on a choice. "Do you want to see something," she asked playfully. She likely realized that the word 'no' wasn't in his vocabulary right then and there.

"Don't move Frank. I'll be right back." Quickly she rose from the couch and headed towards the washroom.

Wild Discretion – Part 2

Frank couldn't remember ever being this turned on, nervous, frightened or excited before in his life. When she left the room to go to the washroom, Frank stood, unzipped his pants and let his erection escape from its confinement. He had an enormous organ and the euphoric yet thrilling relief he felt as he pulled it free and it slapped flat against his body was paradise.

He didn't need anything more than to stroke it. However, he immediately zipped up and again pulled his shirt low before pretending to relax on the armchair. While he stayed there for what appeared like an eternity, Frank continued squeezing his hand against his rigid erection, running it from his balls to the tip. His heart was beating in anticipation and with uncertainty of what was to come.

He heard her approaching but she paused before the refrigerator. The sound of the refrigerator door opening was followed by the clank of bottles and two caps being removed. She came over to him carrying the two bottles of beer and an envelope.

"Tell me you're ready for another," she asked without letting Frank answer as she moved to set the beer bottle on the table before him. She moved around the coffee table and sat on the sofa, only this time, when Janice sat, she patted the couch in a sign to have Frank come and sit beside her. To Frank, it felt like they were getting ready to look at pictures from her family vacation. Frank was a bit confused yet obediently proceeded to sit beside her.

"Alright," she began. "I'm going to show you something no one...and I mean nobody has ever seen before. So you need to promise me that you'll never, ever reveal this to any other person. Deal?"

"I promise," Frank mumbled, a little scared yet thrilled about the secret she was entrusting him with.

"Now, I mean it," Janice enphasized. "Should I ever hear of this getting out, I'll tell everybody you tried to get physical with me and this is only your way of getting back at me."

"I would NEVER...."

"Ssssh...ssssh...It's OK sweetie," Janice said soothingly. "I realize you would never say anything. I simply need you to realize how serious I am about this. As I said, I've never shown these to anybody and I truly need for you to realize that it will stay between us. It's simply something I think you'd appreciate and I'd love to make you happy. Alright?"

"Of course," Frank said with genuine sincerity. "You have my word. I will never under any circumstance say anything. Regardless of what it is. I promise." And Frank meant it.

"Alright," she said as she started to open the envelope. "My boyfriend didn't just like to watch me smoke. He jumped at any chance to take pictures too. Would you like to see some of them? Does this fish like water?"

"Really? Oh! Amazing," Frank immediately answered, perhaps a bit too restlessly. "I'd love to see a few pictures of you when you were 18." Realizing that Janice might have accepted that as his absence of enthusiasm for a more seasoned lady, he immediately included, "Not that you don't look extraordinary now. You do. I mean...well, you know..."

She detected his embarrassment and tenderly put her hand on his arm. "I understand what you mean. Also, thank you. That means a great deal." Frank thought she was serious. "So," she proceeded. "Would you like to see them?"

She took out a stack of perhaps ten, 6x8 photographs. They were black and white; a color palette Frank had generally appreciated when it came to photos. Janice went to hand them to him and teasingly pulled them back," But there's one condition. You can't look at another photo until I say you can, deal?"

"Deal," Frank replied with enthusiasm and she gave him the envelope.

"Well, you realize I'll need a cigarette for this one," and with that, she tapped out another Sobranie. She placed it seductively between her luscious lips and carried the lighter flame to the tip.

Frank forgot all attempts at discretely watching her and openly gawked, with her full knowledge of his enthusiastic interest, and her happiness as a result of it. She made an incredible exhibition of putting away the lighter and making a show of her smoky exhale, much the same as in Casablanca.

"Alright. You can open the envelope and take a look at the first picture."

Frank stopped himself from opening the envelope like a 6-year-old opening a gift on Christmas Morning. The first picture was of Janice..an 18-year-old Janice. She was adorable! She was wearing a sweater and had a youthful elegant richness punctuated with a dazzling smile. The photograph was taken from the driver's side of a vehicle. There was still sunlight out and Frank could tell that it was taken at Flat Top.

"Wow. Magnificent!" Frank said. "You looked great." Frank could have gone with "Saucy," which was exchangeable back then; however, 'great' appeared more decent.

"Yeah..." she chuckled. "I was great. Ok...now take a look at the following picture."

The following shot changed the energy in the room immediately...at least for Frank. It was an image of Janice holding a Sobranie. She had it balanced against her mouth as though she were waiting for a light. A look of exuberant temptation was in her eye. As Frank turned his head towards her, he saw that same look. She carried the Sobranie to her lips, inhaled so he could see it and exhaled.

"Take a look at the next one now."

Frank did as he was told. In this one, Janice's cigarette was lit and she was simply pulling it away from her lips. He could see the smallest puff of smoke in her mouth and it was evident to him that she was starting to perfect her snap inhales, likely, at her boyfriend's request.

"Goodness. This looks incredible," Frank stated, diverting his look from the image to her and back again.

"Thank you. Now take a look at the next one." They continued this way through four or five more photos, each taken at different times of her smoking. Janice was dragging; Janice was inhaling, and Janice was blowing the smoke at the camera. In one, her lips were pressed together like she was whistling and a fine stream of smoke was just inches away from the camera when the photograph was taken.

"I bet he loved this one the best," Frank said intently. "I figure he would."

"Really? Is that the one you like best? You're a bad boy," she said energetically before she took another hard drag and, sitting only a foot away from him, blew her smoke all over his face. The smell drove him to new depths of want, desire and lust. Frank felt his erection throbbing against his stomach. She kept her gaze and stated, "Now take a look at the following one."

Frank tore away from her hypnotizing look and couldn't believe what he found in the following picture. It was a hand, clearly Janice's, holding a cigarette while laying her other hand on an extremely huge tent rising above a pair of trousers.

"Oh my goodness," Frank murmured.

"Do you like it?"

"Holy shit! Yes!"

"Take a look at the following one then."

There was the same hand and the same cigarette, but in this one, the person's enormous erection had been liberated from his trousers and was standing at attention. The little hand holding the cigarette was wrapped around the thick pole. It looked long and fat and hard in her delicate hand.

Frank gazed at Janice restlessly, burning with wild passion and, she viewed both the fear and stimulating excitement. It matched Frank's undoubtedly, or that was what Frank thought at that moment.

"This is one of the sexiest things I've ever seen," Frank exclaimed. "Stunning."

Frank couldn't take his eyes off it. He stared. Neither of them said a word. Janice was likely thinking about her ex-boyfriend's huge erection and how she had once been 18 and somewhat wild. Frank was imagining that he was sitting by a lady on a sofa while she was showing him photographs of her masturbating a cock. They were both lost each in universes of our own and yet having a similar experience.

Her voice got quieter...raspier. "Now, take a look at the next one."

Frank couldn't believe what he was seeing. There was Janice...that colossal pole stuffed in her mouth as smoke surged from her lips. She was giving him a sensational smoking blowjob. Her eyes were shut with her mouth, taking perhaps 50% of his erection into her mouth. Just as Frank was taking this in, he felt an amazing impact of Janice's exhaled smoke hit his nose. It was so wild, so raw, so consumed with electrifying lust. It was like a jolt of electricity. "Now, do you like this one or the last 'holy shit'," Janice inquired.

"Yes, this one" was all Frank could muster.

"Take a look at the following one. I think you'll like it even more."

She had moved her lips off his organ in this one. They rested against the fat mushroom head. Her mouth was loaded up with smoke which was lit splendidly by the blurring sun in the background. Once more, as Frank lost himself in the picture, he inhaled the sweet exhaled smoke originating from Janice's mouth that she had pointed towards him.

"Ok...now the last one. Are you ready?" Frank nodded. "Then proceed."

Frank moved the last photo to the top of the stack and there it was. Cum. It was cum. What's more, lots of it; all over Janice's face. She had her mouth open and loaded up with smoke. Hot spunk was dripping from her cheeks. There were drops in her hair and her lips surrounding the smoke were wet and shimmering. A lovely, sweet 18-year-old young lady covered in thick cum.

"That is hot, isn't it" Janice stated, her face nearly touching Frank's. "So, you like this one too?"

"Yes."

"Does it turn you on?"

"Incredibly."

"Do I turn you on?"

Frank turned to face her. Her lips were shaking. He was trembling like a dry leaf in a whirlwind. For a moment or two, all Frank could hear were the beats of his heart. "More than you know." He stammered in wild excitement.

"Is your cock hard," she murmured. Frank didn't have the foggiest idea what to say.

"Is it?" she asked again. "Is your cock hard for me?" And with that, she blew smoke in his face once more, vigorously breathing out a thick cloud that wrapped around him. "Let me know. Is your cock hard for me?"

"Yes. My cock is hard for you, Janice. So hard. I'm so fucking hard."

"Tell me once more. Is your cock hard for me? Tell me your cock is hard for me," she said practically asserting her seductive dominance.

"Yes! Oh! God yes! My cock is so hard for you. For you!"

"Would you like me to touch your cock," she asked. "Would you like to show me how hard your cock is and have me touch it? Do you need me to smoke for you while I stroke your huge dick?"

"Yesss," Frank murmured, more turned on and harder than he ever felt possible. He was burning in the lust of hellfire.

"Do it. Show it to me. I need to see it. If it's not too much trouble I need to see your cock."

Frank started to fumble as her trembling hands undid his pants...his hands were shaking as he looked into her eyes trying to see a sign to show that this was what she truly needed. He was as hard as he had ever been. As he pulled his shirt up, the head of his cock popped up over his pants.

"Ohhhh...." she murmured. "No doubt about it."

This show of approval did wonders for his libido. He stood up, gradually undid his pants and pulled them down past his hips. His package wrapped up in his underwear, was under the wide-eyed investigation of Janice as she looked up and down the length of his throbbing erection.

Frank was breathing faster and saw that Janice was too. They remained like that for a minute, Frank standing before her in his underwear and she looking.

"Would I be able to see it," she said quietly.

Frank grabbed hold of the band of his underwear, pulled it away from his body, and gradually down, each inch uncovering a greater amount of his throbbing pole. Frank saw a slight flickering on the head. Pre-cum. He was so hard in sensational temptation and wild lust.

As he moved the band lower, he could hear Janice mumble, "Yes." Finally, he reached his balls and afterward rolled the underwear down to meet his jeans, by his ankles.

"You, young fellow, have a wonderful penis."

Perhaps it was "penis" or the earnestness with which she said it. He began to giggle and she did too. Frank thought the existing silliness, apart from everything else, hit them at the same time. Rather than their laughter making them reconsider it created a decent, fun-loving mood. What's more, it indicated that they were both prepared to play.

"Sit down," Janice stated, motioning him to sit beside her. "Lie back."

Frank leaned on his back was against the couch. Janice grabbed her pack of Sobranies and the ashtray which she set on the table to one side. She needed to lean over Frank to reach them and as she did her dangling robe brushed against his exposed erection. Frank jumped in excitement.

"Uh oh, sorry," she mischievously said as she moved back, brought her feet up under her legs and positioned herself to his side. Her robe was still clamped tight around her chest, but as she sat it rose up her leg, completely exposing her thigh. She was suddenly far less a lady and more a young girl.

Detecting his restlessness at being exposed like this before her, she said. "Relax. This is about you feeling good, alright? I need you to feel better. You like to feel better, don't you?"

Frank wanted to. Frank did. Frank was.

"Yes. I like to feel better."

"Would it feel great for me to touch your cock again," she inquired.

"Yes."

"Yes, what?"

"Yes. It would feel great for you to touch my cock again."

"So touch it. Touch it for me."

Frank began to gradually run his trembling fingertips along his extremely hard cock. His fingers were icy cold, he shivered as the warmth of his cock felt the chills of his fingertips, and goosebumps wreaked havoc all over his skin. Frank was quite proud of his size and knew by the expression on Janice's face that she was getting intensely aroused by what she saw. Though it took all his self control not to roughly grasp his dick, stroke it quickly and cum all over, both of them refrained. The ecstatic thrilling moments demanded sensuality...not sexuality.

"That feels better, isn't that right? Mmm...beyond any doubt it looks great. I love it," Janice said enthusiastically and after that with a coy smile added, "What can I do to help Frank Mayhem?" As she said this, she was carrying a new Sobranie to her lips. They both knew precisely what she could, and would, do to help.

"Would you like me to smoke for you," Janice asked mischievously. "Will you play with your enormous cock if I do? Do you need that? Do you need me to smoke for you?" She had the lighter in her grasp. She held it provocatively like a spice girl and had placed it loosely between her full luscious lips.

"Oh, God yes."

"Tell me."

"I need you to smoke for me." Frank swallowed hard at his confessions. "Please...Janice, I need it. Please smoke for me... I need it. I want to stroke my cock while you smoke. I fucking want to watch you smoke while I stroke," Frank breathed, totally surrendering to the urge, crave and longing to his wild and raw desires. He was in a euphoric state where fantasy bridged reality.

Frank lustfully stared as she breathed life into the fire and guided it to the tip of her long Sobranie. He instinctively snaked his hand to the base of his throbbing pole again and gradually stroked upward, covering the head and gradually moving it down once more. Janice drew hard, the orange spark of her cigarette turning brighter through her incredibly long drag. She breathed in completely before breathing out with sheer intent, focusing a tight stream of smoke from his chest to his erection that skipped off his body and lingered for a moment before drifting away.

"Yessss," Frank murmured. "So hot. So fucking hot." Janice took another cheek hollowing drag as she kept her eyes stuck to his hand languidly moving from the base to the head and back once more. Her exhale this time was focused directly on his shaft, the smoke twirling around its length and his hand. Frank stroked somewhat faster, moving his hips up a bit to match his strokes.

She leaned away from him to tap the ash from her Sobranie into the ashtray on the table and Frank saw that her robe was now looser around the top. As she twisted around, her extended finger applying a firm tap to the half-smoked Sobranie, Janice looked over her shoulder and saw his eyes devouring her magnificent breasts. Still leaning over with her eyes never leaving his little yet overwhelming thrill, she delicately grasped her robe and gave a gentle, steady pull to the fabric, gradually uncovering her succulent, juicy and ample tit...the fabric deliberately covering her nipple. Frank stroked faster. Janice chuckled.

"Did you like that?" she purred, nodding subtly toward her abundant bosom.

"Yes."

A grin spread over her face as she pulled her robe back further, now uncovering the top of her areola which was a rich brown; thick and huge. Frank stroked faster.

"Ok....tell me this," she said while settling herself beside him on the couch. She was on her knees which made Frank gaze toward her and asked, "Do you like this as well?"

With that, she leaned in slightly, took a tremendous drag, breathed in firmly and deeply and once the smoke was settled in her lungs rapidly took another. Coming to the opening of her robe, Janice cupped the underside of her tit, pulled it free and exhibited it completely to him. As she did this, she moved her face towards him and washed him with a huge amount of exhaled smoke.

"Oh, fuck..." was all Frank could say under those ecstatic and staggering moments.

Janice didn't utter a single word as she delicately and gradually started rubbing her hand over her bosom. She took another drag as Frank increased the pace on his shaft. After executing a perfect quick inhale, she guided her exhale towards her hardened nipple, squeezing it as the smoke achieved its objective. She groaned.

"Do you love my tits?" Janice teased.

"I love them," Frank whispered, his voice brimming with lustful desire.

"I love your cock. That package is huge and hard. Do you feel good as you stroke your hard cock to my huge tits?" Janice asked as she took another drag and blew her exhale at his face with more intensity. The smell was arousing him in a way he'd never experienced before. It was transporting him to an eternal bliss that appeared to move in slow motion, filling his senses and driving his desire higher than ever. Frank couldn't answer his seductive tormentor. Frank was lost in the moment.

"Tell me you love stroking your cock to me," Janice nearly pleaded.

"I love stroking my cock to you, Janice. I'm so fucking hard only for you. This is so fucking hot...incredible...I...I..."

Frank couldn't express his tempting thoughts. His hand began moving faster, as she started working her tit harder, holding it and squeezing it tight. She put the nearly extinguished cigarette in her full lips, and afterward, clenching it between her teeth, moved her free hand to uncover her other tit. She started rubbing them as one, each hand melding the delicate tissue before coming to together on her now exceptionally hard, enormous nipples and squeezing them hard enough to clearly push the limits between pleasure and pain. She pulled a drag on the Sobranie, breathed in deeply and breathed out just as sharply out her nose, the smoke driving down towards her now erratic hands as Frank stroked his dick wantonly.

She took another hard drag while dangling the now drained cigarette from her lips, then pulled it away, turning quickly toward the ashtray to put it out before rapidly taking another, lighting it, dragging hard and turning back towards Frank, the top of her robe completely open and her enormous breasts completely exposed, her exhaled smoke wafting against Frank's stomach.

Frank was desperate to grab her. He wanted to pull her close to him and feel her enormous tits squeezed against his face. He yearned to take one of her thick nipples and suck it hard; giving her the sensual torment she clearly appreciated. But Frank couldn't.

So far, they hadn't had any genuine body contact whatsoever and he wasn't going to make the first move. Janice was the conductor of this train and Frank was delightfully glad to be along for the ride.

Janice moved up next to him, tucking her legs in and sitting on her knees, she settled herself to his side so he was gazing toward her, her tits full and draping only a few feet from his face. Looking into his eyes, she took a hard drag, breathed in forcefully and leaned her head back, holding the smoke deep into her lungs before blowing a tuft of smoke into the air with a sound of contentment.

Frank had slowed the pace of his hand on his cock and started a moderate rhythm. He wanted this to last.

With her head still tilted back, she promptly took another drag, breathed in slowly, deeply and audibly, and then bent forward until her face was about a foot from his. She started breathing out gradually, the smoke increasing in volume as it left her lungs, as she guided it with pressed together lips all over his face, giving close attention to his nose. Frank breathed in deeply, taking as much of her smoke as he could and started rubbing his erection faster.

Without moving, she took another cheek-emptying drag, played out a hard snap and quickly took another. She reached out and touched his chin, aligning his mouth to hers. This was the first time when they'd had genuine physical contact and a shock ran through Frank's spine. This time, her exhale had one target...Frank's mouth. She leaned in and blew a fine stream past his lips, her face now just inches from his. Frank breathed it in like it was life giving, feeling it fill his lungs. He held it for a minute and let it escape from his body. The smoke moved before Janice's face and he could see her inhale profoundly.

"Now me," Janice murmured, holding the Sobranie to his mouth. Without question, Frank dragged hard and attempted to match her dimension of sexiness as he blew the smoke towards her face. She inhaled it deeply, reclined and started gyrating her hips. She leaned forward slowly and with a dazed look whispered, "Stunning!"

Her eyes trailed down his stomach to see his hand rhythmically stroking his hardened erection. While she watched his hand move up and down his pole Frank watched her carry her Sobranie to her lips and suck the smoke into her lungs, breathe out of her nose with an audible sigh followed by another drag, her eyes never leaving his pole.

Then, she turned towards him and with the smoke still in her mouth, moved her face just inches from his. Janice held it as though it was water and opened her mouth wide. The white smoke appeared to be suspended in time. It gradually swirled yet didn't attempt to escape. Janice held the smoke in her lungs for what seemed like forever before drawing close to his face and covering him with the smell of sex.

She murmured, "Jack your dick."

Frank did. Harder and quicker. She took another drag, this time concentrating on guiding her exhale right into Frank's nose. Frank groaned and her breathing grew heavier. She then took a deep twofold drag, held it for one minute and her face just inches from his forcefully stated, "Fuck yeah. Work that cock," a mass of swirling smoke coming out with her words.

Something about hearing Janice state "Fuck," nearly pushed Frank over the top. He needed to drive his tongue into her mouth. He wanted to grab her...take her. But, he didn't.

She had more to lose if anybody discovered their tryst and Frank assumed that was a choice for her. What's more, at this moment, she needed to watch Frank stroke his cock. And, that was enough for Frank.

Janice had power-smoked her last Sobranie so she moved away towards the ashtray. Frank wasn't overly stressed, yet still confident, that she would light another. With her back to him, Frank heard the sound of her tapping the base of the package to pull out a smoke and the flick of the lighter. Frank kept stroking his cock, feeling almost like he was a voyeur who was getting off without being seen. Before lighting the Sobranie, she turned her head to him and grinned, her eyes moving down to his stone-hard dick and back to meet his eyes. Frank was certain all she saw was lust.

With her face in profile, she provocatively carried the fire to the tip, very much aware of the impact her show was having on Frank. Her exhale was backlight from as yet gleaming yet calm TV and kept up the perfect cone until it scattered in a fog over the room.

She put the lighter down on the table and moved back towards him. Just this time she slid towards the end of the lounge chair, so she was looking directly down on his dick. She gazed for a minute and then looked at him, took a drag and, keeping her eyes secured to his, curved her mouth and dropped her head to blow a surge of smoke at his pole. She grinned, dragged again and this time turned her face so she could focus her exhale on her objective. When the smoke moved over his body, Frank stroked faster. It was amongst the most sensual things he'd ever seen.

"That looks great, doesn't it?" she asked, knowing what his answer would be. "You like stroking your cock for me, isn't that right?

"So much," Frank whimpered.

And afterward, with a voice that was part maternal and part vixen, she asked, "Would you like to cum?"

Frank didn't react. He couldn't. Hearing her say that was the culmination of the many occasions he'd cum with her in his fantasies. Frank was confused.

"You do, don't you," she stated, this time significantly more vixen than matron. She took a long, hard drag, breathed in gradually and without breathing out inclined towards him and stated, "And I do as well. I need you to cum." She then gradually, enchantingly blew her smoke over his eyes, down his nose and blew the remainder of it into his open, hungry mouth.

Her lips were now just inches from his. She pulled once more, the tip shining cherry red, breathed in strongly and drove the smoke into his mouth.

"Yes. Do it. Work your fucking cock," Janice begged.

To hear her talk like this, to act this way, to smoke as she did was too much. Frank could feel his cock start to throb and his balls to tighten. He groaned.

"Yes, baby...do it for me. I need to see it. I need to see you cum," Janice gasped. She started hitting her cigarette over and over. Drags, inhales and exhales were as one as she hung over his face, the smoke thick between them and they each fell further into the profundities of animalistic and lustful fulfillment. Frank's hand was now a haze as he siphoned his cock harder and faster than he could ever remember. He lifted his hips and felt the well-known ascent of an approaching climax. This was unique. It was coming from a place he'd never before experienced. It was profound and obscure and had conquered him completely. He was in a condition of complete orgasmic pleasure while submerging himself in her smoky world.

"I'm cumming," Frank murmured. "Oh, God...I'm cumming...I'm cumming...."

Janice gave herself wholeheartedly to his cock. She grabbed it from him and drove her mouth deep down the shaft, pumping her hand all over, coordinating the movement with her bobbing head. Her mouth, hot and wet, felt like eternal bliss. Frank came instantly...huge jets of cum detonated from his dick, again and again as she groaned. Her lips were stuck over the cock head. She attempted to inhale through her nose as his juices filled her hot mouth. Little surges of cum slid down the side of her face. It was the most exceptionally stimulating pleasure moment Frank had ever felt.

As Frank drifted off into a post-coital state that felt like electricity coursing through his veins, Janice gradually brought her mouth off his cock, carried the now little cigarette to her lips, dragged and opened her mouth wide. There in the midst of the moving smoke was his cum, more than he'd ever seen from a masturbating session. She breathed in the smoke and after that with a glimmer in her eye, gulped his load. When it was gone, she gave her lips one final lick and after that, erotically breathed out her smoke toward Frank. In every one of the fantasies, he'd written in his mind, Frank couldn't have hoped for a better ending.

"Thank you," was all Frank could utter. Nothing more needed to be said.

"No," Janice answered. "Thank you." She moved her hand to the side of his face. "I mean that," she said with some seriousness. "Thank you, Frank. By the way, I'm Annie J Mar aka Janice Jayne. It was a great pleasure spending quality time with one of my most ardent readers."

Lethal Attraction

It was the time of sixth century India; states after states, kingdoms after kingdoms were rampaged by the ruthless King of Magadha, Maharaja Vikrama. His skilled military expeditions, brutality and hunger to conquer the whole of India soon made him the Rajadhiraja (Ruler of Rulers) in the whole Eastern India. And soon, opponent Kingdoms joined hands to safeguard their interests against the cruel king. The master schemer devising the comprehensive plan to take down the kingdom of Magadha was minister Vatsayana of Jodhpur, Rajasthan. He assigned his extensively trained Vishkanya, Mohini for this job.

On a royal wedding in one of his minister's places, Maharaja Vikrama met Mohini. And it was just like love at first sight for the youthful and commanding ruler. Maharaja Vikrama was adamant, hard-hearted, dominant and ruthless when it came to expand his empire, but when it came to meet Mohini and spend some quality time with her far away from the war, the burden of decision making, surprisingly, he was quite polite, patient with Mohini.

He loved fulfilling her demands and Vikrama found pleasure, liberty and empowerment to be in Mohini's control. He was severely infatuated with her, which was the magic that was spelled upon the king by the gorgeous and seductive Mohini.

Not only was he possessed by her beauty, he was also mesmerized by her quick wit, political knowledge and matters related to the exquisite art of seduction. And soon, they got married and Mohini became Maharani Mohini. Sensual and romantic nights became the norm of his royal bedroom. With the expertise of a paramour, Mohini taught her new king the art of tease and denial, foreplay, and the exquisite art of pleasuring a woman.

Gone were the nights of fast and savage sex like tossing a woman on the bed and pounding her like a bull. With Mohini, Vikrama learned the game of seducing the mind before seducing the body. But this was a roller-coaster ride in which Mohini always held the steering wheel.

For the first time ever in his mortal life, the Maharaja learned how he can efficiently utilize his mouth and tongue to worship any woman's body. Maharani Mohini trained him on how to worship a lady with his tongue in the junction of her legs. Like an outstanding bright student, excited to learn new things, Maharaja Vikrama proved his worth to his beautiful Maharani, adhering to her explicit demands word by word. Right from the initial days of their happy marriage and sexual intimacy, she led the way.

Eventually, it was an integral part of their thrilling sensual encounters that the Maharaja's head was to be buried in the junction of his Maharani's legs to initiate the play. Habituated to this new submissive task, Maharaja Vikrama was always anxious to please Maharani Mohini by this prelude. If being a visionary, ruthless, and victorious king was his primary nature, then pleasuring his soulmate with his mouth and tongue turned into his second. And undoubtedly and unquestionably, the Maharaja cherished surrendering himself to his Lady as much as the Maharani did in conquering and subjugating him, physically and mentally.

Tirelessly, the Maharaja went through infinite hours to pleasure her sexy and lush body. He worshipped his seductive Goddess, his Maharani with soft, delicate kisses showering oral tributes all over her. He was overwhelmed by the delicious delight of pleasuring his Goddess.

The passionate excitement of caressing of his sex Goddess consumed the Maharaja's senses like a potent aphrodisiac. He spent countless, delightful vast hours devouring the Maharani's exquisite juices from the heavenly adobe in between her legs. Soon his needs on his bed transformed into pleasuring his Maharani and sex Deity instead of his own orgasms.

Whenever the Maharaja entered his kingly bedroom after a day of hard and brainstorming decisions for conquering new kingdoms, Vikrama witnessed Mohini wearing an exquisite sari that revealed her irresistible seduction rather than shrouding it, that exhibited her stunning curves and rather than concealing it. Soon consumed by savage lusts and wild desires to please his

Maharani, his submissive mind would provoke him to ignore every single masculine qualities and his eager mouth would be left drooling in intense, urgent wants. As his cravings just fixated on pleasuring his Maharani by his mouth, she cherished to tease his ultimate temptation.

After a short pursuit and hide and seek inside the bedroom, with extensive commitments of more jewelry and sophisticated attires, Vikrama accomplished his objective and his head would be buried in the middle of her legs, mouth on her pussy lips, and her long, slinky, sexy legs folded around his shoulders. In his servile position, Vikrama realized getting intensely stirred and exceptionally aroused. It took colossal restraint on his part not to explode against the bed as Mohini fed him her flavorful vaginal juices.

Once in a while, depending upon her state of mind, Mohini would allow him to perform additional kissing on the glorious pits of her womanhood after she was done with her squirting. These were the occasions when Mohini permitted Vikrama to sniff and taste her abundant butts after devouring the honey from her juicy pussy as he delicately lapped. Then again, it turned out to be progressively harder for Vikrama not to release in the bed as his desperation for sexual liberation reached its peak; Vikrama rubbed himself against the bed his wild sexual excitement, getting closer and closer to his own climax.

Vikrama hardly understood that the more time he spent offering his oral tributes to his Maharani, the less regular were his sexual intercourses with her. In any case, it entirely depended on Mohini when or how she would allow him to penetrate her. Usually, when she was perfectly satisfied by her royal slave's oral tributes, she would simply roll over and nod off. And as always, Vikrama just craved to proceed with his soft caresses on Mohini's attractive body with his entire heart and soul.

If he was the crowned king in his kingdom, she was the uncrowned and undisputed MAHARANI of the bedroom. Since inside the bedroom, Vikrama was engaged with one-sided lovemaking and his very own sexual needs were hardly fulfilled. Thus, he was in a state of constant excitement, induced arousal, and extreme horniness. He desperately yearned for her, always, yet was experiencing lesser sexual intercourses. In a way never sensed and experienced before, the more he lusted and yearned for her the more overpowering and intense was his obsession.

In this manner, Mohini proclaimed that her body was accessible, but just on her terms. Vikrama's cravings to please his royal consort surpassed all boundaries compelling him to acknowledge her absolute dominance. It appeared the less she permitted him for a regular intercourse, the stronger and fiercer were his passions and arousals for her.

During the day, he was a skilled military strategist, a powerful ruler, and a noble king making hard decisions about his kingdom, conquests and welfare of his subjects. Be that as it may, during the night, in his kingly bedroom, he had authority, dominance, and powers no more, and his worthy wants focused on pleasuring his Goddess regardless of how humiliating they were. He didn't expect such a tremendous turnaround in his relationship when he married Mohini, yet when it gradually began, he was too weak to stop the inevitable descent.

Always in the night, Maharaja Vikrama would enter the bedroom with wild lust filled in his heart and aspired to pound his soulmate with his masculinity, his manhood. Alas! Mohini hardly allowed him the luxury of sexual intercourse. Every time, she just permitted his tongue in her. "Your MAHARANI should never ask," that was what Mohini asserted once. And, Vikrama's sole existence was to serve his QUEEN, Maharani Mohini.

One day, after spending tedious hours taking hard and crucial decisions for the betterment of his subjects and planning the expansion of his kingdom, Vikrama vowed to conquer his QUEEN and consummate the night with a series of savage, wild and carnal sex. On his way home to his kingly room, his hard and leaking erection never stopped poking in his mind the desperation of his lustful needs. As he entered the bedroom, he saw Mohini sitting and posing before a mirror, applying a few Ayurvedic moisturizers on her beautiful face.

A translucent, sophisticated silken robe parting in the mid-section, exhibited her long, sexy legs. Her robe was unbuttoned at the top, partly uncovering her abundant bosoms. She looked so gorgeous in the full moon moonlight, that Vikrama immediately forgot his oath of penetrating his Maharani. As his heart got filled with savage and unquenchable desires, he simply wanted to worship his Maharani by his tongue.

Turning enchantingly towards him, Mohini allowed her elegant attire to tumble from her shoulder teasing all of his sexual fantasies as she uncovered her whole lush body. Vikrama's knees weakened, as he craved for nothing more than to bury his head in the junction of her legs and shower his oral tributes in the pit of her womanhood.

"How did it go today?" Mohini teased as she gradually brushed her long, dense hair. Instantly, her exotic voice dried his throat, his heart skipped a beat and his expressive tongue dictating commands for his officers and subjects was speechless fumbling for words.

"Fine…" Vikrama stammered. Mohini chuckled mischievously; she knew how her body was toying with the king's mind, exciting him and decided to continue teasing a little longer. She parted her legs slightly; gave him an alluring smile and he was in her control. Gradually, extending one leg in an enticing way, she caught him drooling like a puppy as his eyes got locked on the rich pink spot.

"My Maharaja, my beloved husband, I love these silk robe. I need a few of these," Maharani Mohini demanded. The powerless Maharaja thought for a minute to discuss with her about her extravagant lifestyle, about how her excessive demands for costly dress and jewelry was taking a toll on the royal treasury. Then, as she lifted one leg onto the chair arm, grabbing it with her hands, exhibiting her juicy pink spot completely, the shaky Maharaja lost all sense of reasoning and hungered to devour her rich juices.

"Sure! I'll tell the dressmaker regarding your requirements," Vikrama murmured as he brought himself down to his knees before her. His desperate arms were begging to caress her legs; his hungry lips restless to tribute his Maharani at her marvelous pit. There he was, kneeling before his queen, his royal consort with the sole ambition to serve her. Towering above him and above his bowing head, Maharani Mohini chuckled approving his surrender.

With trembling hands the Maharaja caressed the lustrous thighs of the Maharani; she shivered; his fingers were so damn cold. Her eyes glittered seeing his royal slave breathing heavily. Mohini kept her legs squeezed firmly, denied him from voyaging upward; she teased in a demeaning tone, "What is it that my dear husband seeks so desperately?"

"Please," Vikrama mumbled. "Please...I just want to kiss you...please," His shaking tone and trembling lips had lost their kingly status to the seductive teases of the Maharani.

"Kiss me? Just kiss me. Your wife is practically naked before you and you just want to kiss me?" Mohini teased further.

"Please." Vikrama's voice was strained. "Please, give me a chance to kiss you. The spot where you love to be kissed so much," he desperately pleaded, getting almost teary and the volcanic desire consuming his earthly senses.

"My Maharaja, you are my husband. Don't you think you should never kneel before me? Shouldn't I be on my knees before you?" Mohini teased seductively.

Rather than demonstrating substantial arrogance and significant protest to her taunting, the authoritarian ruler couldn't understand the mind games of his spouse. Consequently, a wave of submission conquered him further.

"Please! Give me a chance to kiss you." His lips frantically pleaded for his reward, but they were stopped by her strong thighs.

"Kiss me? That's it? Why shouldn't my Maharaja demand what he needs? Not begging on his knees like a second-rate slave." Mohini lifted Vikrama's head with her hand grasping his hair. Her expressive eyes glared down at him seeing her very own reflection in his. "Is that your wish? You sure you don't need anything more."

"Please! My Maharani! I want to worship you just like the way you love. I just want to love you in the extraordinary way that brings you heavenly delight." The Maharaja begged.

Maharani Mohini released his tangled hair the manner in which an adult would do to a child and strolled to the bed. He lay on his knees, watching and impatiently waiting.

"Come, my beloved husband. Come to your wife," reclining on the bed Mohini commanded her royal slave spreading her legs enticingly. Vikrama rose up to oblige to her commands.

"No," she strongly ordered him in a commanding tone as he took his first kingly stride. Vikrama froze immediately, bewildered by her authoritative commands. "If your craving is so desperate, prove your worth. Crawl to me and prove how desperate you're to please me."

A sudden furious shock of outrage fired in Vikrama's eyes, the recklessness of her authoritarian voice devastating the last piece of pride whatsoever of what was left in him. He would have chopped off that person's tongue had he or she dared to command him in that humiliating decree, he would have shoved red-hot iron stick in that person's eyes had he or she demonstrated such audacity. Battling with the burden of his irresistible lust, his mind surrendered to her words. Before entering the bedroom, he pledged to ram his royal consort with his manhood to enjoy the ecstatic pleasure rides of the highest heavens; perhaps, if he could have done that but now his eyes were focused on the favored orifice between her legs.

There were no indications of any masculinity and manly conduct in Vikrama as he watched the enticing showcase of a temptress before him. Mohini put a cushion underneath her back lifting up her blessed juicy hole to be served by her royal slave, uncovered her delicious, succulent breasts and parted her legs further displaying her magnificent abode in between her legs.

Witnessing his prize was so compelling and irresistible for Vikrama that without pondering the results of his activities he started to crawl towards his desirable objective. Never in his life had he done such a demeaning demonstration, yet the vision of his most deserving prize constrained him and obstructed his sense of reasoning and pride. When his lips and tongue touched the heavenly hole, Mohini shivered in ecstasy and dominance.

Vikrama rolled, twisted, shoved his tongue in and out of her pleasure spot endeavoring to satisfy his wife; she moaned and delighted the stirring sensations of the ninth heaven when waves after waves of passion rippled through her, streaming down the precious juices that the kingly slave so greedily devoured.

"That's my slave. But I'll have to train you more. You'll have to learn." Mohini stated and nodded off.

The following day, the powerless Maharaja could hardly give any consideration to his royal duties. His body was attending the royal meetings; however, his mind and soul continued wandering in his bedroom. His contentions were too overpowering to even let him focus on his professional duties. Outrage, disappointment, and shame consumed one part of his conscience recognizing that as a rich, royal, and commanding man and a devoted husband he should demand from his wife all the marital benefits. If he somehow happened to be denied, he should toss his queen onto the bed and thrust mightily into her exhibiting who wore the pants in their relationships.

But, the other half of his mind was baffled by erotic excitement and endless delight. As Vikrama recalled his last night's demeaning chores, he was excessively stimulated and considered how the expertise of his tongue gave his queen three overwhelming orgasms and he devoured her delicious juices thrice after he worshipped the Holy Grail in between her legs. By and by, his lustful needs to peak in his wife's womanhood were dismissed as serving his royal consort, his Maharani, was his ultimate goal.

Yet, he understood something. His savage lust for her was so colossal and extraordinary that he always craved for her. He required her approval and consent to be intimate with his Maharani and he could go to any extent for that regardless of how humiliating that might be, regardless of how his wife treated him like a slave for her very own joys. His submissive mind constantly wanted to surrender everything to his wife just to taste the deliciousness of her glorious pussy. He was relieved from the agony of debasement. Mohini, on the other hand, simply cherished her freedom to tease and dominate her husband while he was on his knees begging to kiss her on her favored pink spot.

That day also, after attending to his long and tedious kingly duties and brainstorming strategically on his upcoming conquests, he was once again filled up with savage wants. With firm intent, Vikrama resolved to approach Mohini and demand the fulfillment of his own sexual needs, his orgasms during an intercourse. He again vowed to act like the potent man he was and demonstrate his masculinity as a king and as a man.

Marching with the glory like a king after a day-long battle, Maharaja Vikrama entered the spacious royal bedroom only to discover that his wife had just come out of the shower. Without recognizing his presence, the gorgeous, seductive and manipulative Maharani stood marginally bent over, stripped, drying her hair. The exhibitions were unbelievable, truly sensual and extremely stirring even more than before; the captivating sight of her hemispherical scoop like ass hypnotized his senses.

Within moments, he had forgotten his impotent masculine vows. Vikrama stood at the threshold absolutely entranced by the seductive demonstration.

Vikrama observed enthusiastically as Mohini shook her hair dry. His legs were debilitated and he was losing all sense of reasoning to his volcanic lusts. Her amazing buttocks shook rhythmically as she toweled her long hair dry. As Mohini completed her undertakings, her eyes, at long last, caught him devouring her seduction. With a dominating tone and a demeaning look, she comprehended what Vikrama's center of fascination was. She kept herself steady like an experienced paramour and an expert manipulator for long minutes to capture her slave in her captivating web. Vikrama's eyes barely moved from her wonderful pussy and fleshy buttocks. Seductively, the Goddess bent further, gradually, while witnessing the tremendous impact of her lovely ass on him. She chose to conclude the tempting display as she turned towards him, covering herself with the towel.

"You wish something, my Maharaja?" Mohini asked Vikrama in a mortifying tone because she knew he would be too powerless to speak after such a provocative tease. Like an angel from the heaven, she walked towards the bed and dropped the towel exhibiting her attractive feminine assets. Vikrama attempted to move toward her yet was halted just by a wave of her hand.

As she spread her sexy legs showing her blessed orifice in between her legs, the Maharani mockingly indicated the floor. In an urgent need to release his servile obligations, Vikrama immediately bowed and crept to the bed. She gestured him to join her on the bed where his tongue tasted the delicious prize. Gone were his masculine promises and habits, as he began to touch her sensitive opening with the extraordinary ability his wife had taught him. Wrapping her alluring legs over his shoulders, her hands stuffed his head on her heavenly gates as he proceeded with his obligations submissively. His dexterous pleasuring drove her to overwhelming orgasmic delights. Vikrama wanted to fulfill his desire by his masculinity rather he ended up pleasuring his Maharani by his tongue. This left him as horny as before with an edgy desire to climax in his bed. At long last, when Mohini was happy with Vikrama's oral tributes, she pushed him away. In his feeling of still discontent desire, his slobbering lips still lusted for the skin to skin touch and sought after her as she gradually rolled aside.

"Are you still hungry to serve your Maharani, my beloved husband?" Mohini taunted Vikrama once more, demonstrating him who was in control. With his mouth still lubed to her heavenly gates devouring the residues, Vikrama stared up at his Maharani. The gorgeous Maharani chuckled wickedly as she glared at her slave. With his mouth and lips covered with her precious serum, Vikrama admitted his need to perform his obligations as he nodded.

"Then serve your Maharani as she wants." Mohini commanded sternly.

Her wants were his commands and as she finished commanding her slave, she rolled on her stomach. The abundant mounds of her velvety buttocks showed up before his face. His masculine stature was torn apart, his honor battling his wild desires. Vikrama gazed at the delicate, perfect hemispherical scoops, his mouth was drooling. He remembered the images of his beautiful Maharani bending over after the shower. An evil desire crushed him and he realized the desperate cravings to worship her bootylicious ass.

As far as he could realize, Vikrama began to snake his tongue from his mouth and tenderly licked one of her delicate ass cheeks. His uncontrollable desires and lustful wants conquered his musings and he tried to discover the narrow fissure with his tongue. With adoring hands, Vikrama parted the gorgeous ass cheeks of his Maharani and explored the profundities inside by his tongue. Mohini pushed back at him, she shivered with lust-filled dominance entrapping his tongue deep inside her fissure. All of a sudden, as he demonstrated his unquestionable and devotional commitment, his balls exploded against the bed and he climaxed intensely.

The Maharani permitted her slave some more time to kiss and offer his oral tributes as he descended from the peaks of his sexual excitement, he just experienced. Vikrama fell asleep with his mouth glued to her ample ass mounds.

From that day onwards, his manliness was diminished distinctly to just a name. After ordinary routine work when he would return at night, he would crawl to his Goddess to perform his servile tasks dedicatedly. Her unquenchable desires and selfish wants were his commands, absolute orders. At that point, she was the authority not only in the bedroom, but in addition to the whole family and royal decisions. She was the lady in boots in the kingdom, with the former man in boots without a spine crawling at her feet like a humble servant, yearning to follow all orders.

Vikrama who demonstrated his valor in conquering new kingdoms was now performing womanly tasks like washing Mohini's robes, clothes and sari and helping her to dress. He was absolutely manipulated and toyed regardless of who he was. As he continued with his tasks, if Mohini was in the mood, she would then let him offer oral tributes to one of her precious holes. During the night, the slave would wash her feet, kiss them dry, sucking each toe, gradually working his direction upward. Her lovable body was the only sacred shrine where he wished to offer his tributes anytime and without fail.

One night, the royal slave was restrained under his kingly bed in his luxurious chamber. The Maharani had invited one of her more potent and masculine subjects to the royal bedroom to experience the ecstatic pleasures that every woman yearns for. The subject proved his worth to the Maharani as he pounded deep inside her like a bull breeding a cow, like a horse breeding a mare. The euphoric delights of orgasmic pleasures escaped through her mouth in the form of uproarious slutty moans as if she was getting exorcised. Lying beneath the bed, the once-upon-a-time conqueror listened to his Maharani's moans as he witnessed the bed rock and shake like a tragic earthquake.

He impatiently waited to consummate the unthinkable tragedy of his life, eagerly awaited to please his royal owner. When the potent subject left, depleted, exhausted and pleased to satisfy the queen of the realm, the former ruler acknowledged his new demeaning royal duty, CLEANSING his QUEEN of another's seed.

Sultry Fear

That was a long-needed vacation for her. Lisa had excused herself from all household and university work and all she planned was to cherish some relaxing time at her parental countryside manor. Throughout the following two days, she had very little work to do at her home and all Lisa craved was for the weekend to arrive soon.

With a tight schedule of work, her mother couldn't spend any happy get-together time with her throughout the day. However, before leaving for the afternoon, she had requested a cleaning and maintenance of her estate from the neighborhood hardware store and the manager had agreed to her request.

Moreover, Lisa would be at home for the afternoon, so if necessary, she could monitor the maintenance folks to ensure they followed explicit orders. As the week advanced, Lisa was getting seriously on edge and stimulated watching her cam-works, what she did for her ardent followers. Furthermore, her jovial correspondences with her closest companion Bettina about her BDSM experiences never enabled her to settle her nerves.

She had promised herself to abstain from internet dating and cam-work sessions until the successful completion of her university appraisals. However, she couldn't stop herself from searching the web about sexual relationships and hardcore sensual experience stories.

Upon the start of the Villa maintenance work, Lisa was alone in the house, checking out the hunks mowing the lawn, working on the planters, fence, and weeding.

After reading a messier hardcore erotic book on her PC about a horny youthful college girl getting gangbanged at her birthday party, she couldn't resist the temptation of getting turned on by the possibility of various hunks taking a lady.

Maybe, as BDSM, this was also one of her hidden fantasies where she wanted to be firmly taken by a few hunks that would play dirty with her. While becoming mixed up in her own exuberant desires, she thought about whether something was seriously wrong with her.

Yet, with such a significant number of online sites sharing sensual experiences, she consoled herself that presumably there were numerous young girls just like her who clearly fell into her classification. After all, it's absolutely unfair when you hide your true self, isn't?

When she was done with her amorous story, she was so horny that she decided to share some feedback. Eventually, she wrote:

"Once in a while I simply wish that I could encounter several hunky men and really do every one of the fantasies that are shared in this story... I don't have the foggiest idea why I get so turned on by the possibility of different men slamming against a helpless lady. Probably the most burning fantasy is to get all my cavities filled up by some powerful tools as though being air locked. Despite the fact that I've never attempted such a desperate thing, I wouldn't refrain should life introduce such an exciting opportunity."

Reviewing her comment, she decided she was done. She believed that it was presumably the briefest survey and feedback she'd ever composed. She laughed at herself because normally her feedback and comments stretched out to the length of the sexual stories that she read. In addition, she wanted to portray explicit fantasies and situations that she'd prefer to experience if she were the story's character.

She exhaled and strolled to the kitchen from where she pulled out a cucumber. Despite the fact that she realized it wouldn't be the same, she'd at least get a stirring feeling, and in sheer desperation, she rubbed it between her hands to warm it up.

After stripping out of her dress, she lay naked on the floor and thrust the cucumber into her drenched pussy while envisioning a group of studs standing around, jerking off. As she plunged further into her fantasies, she imagined in her mind one of the maintenance hunky men working in the garden, pounding her in between her legs. She began to shove the cucumber all through her pussy and attempted to fuck herself harder with it. She fantasized about two different hunks kneeling down on either side of her, sucking and kneading her nipples. She was attempting to experience an overwhelming climax.

However, it wasn't working. She wasn't able get herself anywhere near what she imagined in her mind. Her urgency developed, enticing her to discharge her passionate juices. Feeling on edge and hopeless, yet horny, she pummeled the cucumber into her pussy hard and played with her succulent tits.

At long last, she chose to forsake her fantasy and strove hard to climax. In spite of the fact that she came hard, she anticipated a more noteworthy sensation. However, she was unable to experience it which at last left her unfilled and frustrated. Disappointed, she threw out the cucumber and retired to her bed for a rest.

Lisa woke up after a few hours. It was nearly evening. As she came to her senses, she was surprised to find that her sheets were off and the shirt that she slipped into before sleeping, was up above her chest uncovering her succulent luscious milk buckets. Hands were feeling her statuesque seductive figure. She realized that her panties were slid down to her ankles. Shocked beyond imaginations, she desperately inhaled to shout. All of a sudden, she was muffled by a hand that was wrapped up with coarse gloves and muffled her voice.

"The bitch is awake," one of the voices murmured in a low filthy tone, and she at long last looked upon her various impassioned takers. Again within a few of moments, another cruel, demanding tone expressed: "Give me her underwear." Accordingly, her eyes widened in fear shuddering in frustration and outrage. Her panties were pulled away from her ankles and were stuffed into her mouth restricting her strenuous attempts to scream.

The three sets of hands viciously moved all over her lush body. Regardless of being pinned down on the bed, she was unbelievably turned on by the brutalities. All of a sudden, it flashed in her mind that these conditions resembled the sensual story she'd read before nodding off.

Desperately she thought: "Am I dreaming? Is it truly happening?" Petrified dread and chills ran up and down her spine, yet she couldn't deny the turn on. She chose to cooperate as long as they didn't want to hurt her. Tragically, in her restraint, she was unable to admit this and so just squirmed as they violated her seductive body.

While numerous fingers squeezed her nipples hard, kneading them brutally, tears streamed from her eyes. However, the equivalent abusing shot thrilling electric desire straight through her pussy. Arching her back and foot on the bed, she desperately attempted to adjust the torments. The fingers tugged her nipples skyward, step by step stretching out her luscious udders. Despite dread seething through her veins, she was exceedingly horny at how her alluring lavish body responded to the violations and maybe wanted some more. A perverted part of her mind gloried in the fact that she was so deviant.

In the event that they had released her of her gagged underwear, she'd be begging for their cocks, urging them to continue with their cruel play. Feeling dizzy and precarious as those hands slid up her inner thighs, she felt two coarse fingers separating her labia and thrusting in her pussy.

"Good Lord! This bitch is enjoying! She's already soaked and ready," an unpleasant voice mumbled, "You like this, don't you whore?"

Lisa's rich body began to respond to the name as the fingers infiltrated her rosebuds. She groaned from her panty-gag. Eventually, those men laughed naughtily as she squirmed in ecstasy possibly requesting more brutalities. Immediately, mouths secured her nipples and sucked her succulent, tasty udders hard while another tongue examined her lavish pussy. She sensed being in indescribable ecstatic paradise and she relaxed for a moment since they were not going to hurt her. Feeling horrendously unbelievable, her revulsions and fears retreated behind the walls of her unrestrained wild desires. As their mouths kept teasing her pussy and sucking on her nipples and areola, Lisa burned again in volcanic desire and shuddered in seething allurement and wild lust.

Once more, with one man's finger attacking and probing the wetness of her pussy, combined with all the oral incitement of the other two, it was inevitable that Lisa would encounter another overwhelming ejaculation. Furthermore, when she climaxed with ecstatic joy, her body arched and shuddered in bliss. She shouted and groaned in wonderful enjoyment.

At last, the men wickedly giggled out loud triumphantly for they realized that they had kindled her inner bitch in heat. As she watched them strip off their garments, she burned with savage wants. Then, one of the men grasped her hips and turned her over, she fought him to their sheer surprise. She received a resounding slap on her hemispherical ass mounds immobilizing her and stopping her rebellion. However, it didn't decrease her excitement.

When they held her hands behind her back, she found that incredibly arousing rather than terrifying. This was something exciting. She was totally vulnerable to the three hunky studs loaded up with potent sperm. Knowing her unguarded state, they removed the panty-gag from her mouth. Giving her only the opportunity to cry out: "Please you don't need to... UMPH!" But her endeavors were all futile and landed on deaf ears. At last, she understood that they'd removed the panty-gag to stuff her mouth with one of their cocks. Within seconds and without wasting any time, that stud began to fuck her luscious mouth and said: "Stop battling it, bitch! Enjoy it!" As he thrust into her throat, she felt as though he was pumping air out from her lungs.

She gagged on that mammoth cock. Feeling a flash of discontent, she thought to advise them: "You don't need to be so unpleasant! I'll cooperate!" But they appeared to gain a great deal of delight out of her helpless and vulnerable state and clearly, she also couldn't have denied it. Lisa felt so frightened that she had no control over her savage wants and lust-filled wishes.

When the hunk released her mouth from his glorious shaft, Lisa coughed spilled heaps of saliva. Then, they lifted her up straddling on one of them who lay on the bed with his thick gigantic fat cock pointing to the roof excitedly waiting to attack her ready and ever delicious pussy.

When they brought her down onto him, she groaned and shouted vigorously. Besides, her tightness deliciously enveloping his hot and erect fuck meat made Lisa become lightheaded from the subsequent joys. As the two groaned in joy and delight, the delicateness and wetness of her pussy sucked him inside her. She understood the regions in her pussy that she was so urgent to encounter. Grabbing her juicy bosoms, he invaded somewhere down in her and she felt as though she were pierced on his extra-large cock. He squeezed her nipples and she whimpered in excitement and delight as he settled himself comfortably beneath her.

All of a sudden, Lisa felt a leather-like belt in her mouth, which she understood to be a gag with a wide round opening. Then, one of the men stuffed her mouth again with his massive powerful cock. She understood that he wanted to get a blowjob from her while his mates would be busy filling her cavities with their fuck meats.

With her hands held behind her back, Lisa had no control over the deep throated blowjob. Understanding this, the strong hunk shoved his way more deeply into her throat, which scared Lisa as she had never attempted gagged on deep throat before.

The hunky man appeared to barely think about her alarming groans and proceeded with his cocky invasion of her throat. Working all through her juicy and warm mouth, pounding further and more profoundly into her throat and finally making her gag was an ordeal. All of a sudden, her attention shifted to certain developments in her butt hole. She shuddered when she felt something vile and long thrusting against her anal pit. Instantly, Lisa's seductive body was crippled in fear when she remembered one of her dreams wherein, she hungered to be air locked in all of her bodily cavities.

She shouted as the cock started squeezing into her butt nugget, stretching the hole with anguishing torment. Detecting her distress, the hunk attacking her virgin ass, applied some lube on his dick and Lisa detected the oily, smooth internal development of the pole in her butthole. Her vocal reverberation got away from her body in groans.

Also, it just vibrated the cock deep siphoning into her mouth, making the hunk groan in electrifying sensation and urging him to fuck her throat with his cock further and deeper. At last, when she had her nose squeezed against his crotch, she smelled the musky powerful damp with sweat fragrance of his body further intensifying her excitement. She was in an insidiously difficult state, yet volcanic desire consumed her body with an ideal blend of agony and delight.

She was not able to decide what was trickier for her, the fuck meat attacking her throat or the fuck pole attacking her virgin tight anal pit. Tears sprang from her eyes flooding her cheeks as all three hunks began their thrilling thrust throughout her body, generating sensational ecstasy, sensual reverberations and pleasure juices.

While her ass burned and clenched in an alluring blend of torment and joy, her pussy felt amazingly great. Furthermore, having a mammoth strong cock stuffed in her mouth just caused her to acknowledge how satisfied she could be. Truth be told, in sheer allurement and bubbling desire she wished, she'd not had the gag in her mouth. She could have demonstrated her greatness with her mouth.

Groaning between thrusting bodies, Lisa sensed the undeniable irritation easing and she was getting encompassed by a significant sentiment of ecstatic delight. Every one of her cavities tightened convulsively as short waves of euphoria shuddered her seductive structure. In spite of the fact that she was not emitting her juices, she just felt like little tremors in preceding a shattering quake. Additionally, she wanted for her significant senses of thrilling joy not to end too soon.

Lisa couldn't think straight, and she couldn't breathe deeply. All she could inhale was the musky sweat-soaked smell of the man's crotch and shaft. All she could concentrate on were the throbbing sensations her seductive body was encountering because of the extraordinary satisfaction of her cavities. Moreover, all she could feel was lubricated cocks moving all through her cavities, strongly pleasuring her.

Most likely, hurting her a bit; however, her joys vanquished the torment with each conceivable development. Lisa edged to her sexual freedom and her body shook in delights of the most elevated paradise. Besides, within seconds of her overwhelming orgasm, she felt a burning tingle entering further inside her pits with each pressurizing thrust. Her clit thrummed against the hunky man underneath her as she rode him. With a shout, she felt herself significantly falling over the edge, each vein in her seductive body tauter in ecstasy as her pits gagged on the poles satisfying her.

One, two, three, in a steady progression, the hunky men orgasmed inside her cavities, first one in her mouth, the second one in her pussy and the third one in her ass; not at the same time yet more or less simultaneously. Moreover, each of the ejaculations drove her further up towards magnificent delight gasping for air. At last, the powerful man pulled himself from her mouth and she fell onto the chest of the man she was riding.

Abruptly, one of the voices murmured in her ears: "Welcome Home, Lisa!" and a chilling wave flushed all through her worn out body. Gathering the last bit of her strength, she pursued the voice, she was entranced to find that it was that of Hugo's. She remembered him as one of her enthusiastic followers on the online adult cam-dating site; the person who had paid her hotel bill when she was on a visit to Paris.

Then again, "Welcome Home, Lisa!" smiled another voice totally shattering her senses. Once more, as she pursued the voice, she petrified in dread to find that it was Nolan's, her twitter friend, who further shouted: "We found your remarks on the online erotic site, and thought you were desperate to have a try at something unusual." As Hugo and Nolan loosened her arms from behind her back, she couldn't expect a more shock from the Pandora box when she gazed at the smiling face before her and discovered Trent, a culinary expert at the same hotel in Paris, where she stayed during her visit.

Lisa was astonished. Her voice trapped in her throat as she shuddered in tension, euphoria and swallowed in air. When she rolled off of Hugo, she was depleted from the marathon session and seeping cum from every one of her pits. As the three men gazed at their triumphant victory, they were confused by her responses, yet they were certain that she could never be furious.

At long last, Lisa approved, "You guys are awesome..., but what brought you here?"

Nicolas answered: "Hugo read your online comments and feedback and he saw your remark on the adult site where you expressed that 'you won't hold yourself back if life presents you with such an amazing chance'. Well, we're the party!"

CPSIA information can be obtained
at www.ICGtesting.com
Printed in the USA
LVHW080906220621
690766LV00002B/294